LOST AND FOUND IN HARLEM

A Ross Agency Mystery

DELIA C. PITTS

ISBN: 1976326753
ISBN 13: 9781976326752
Library of Congress Control Number: 2017914662
CreateSpace Independent Publishing Platform
North Charleston, South Carolina

TABLE OF CONTENTS

Chapter 1
THE ROUGE

The fire at the Auberge Rouge gutted me.

I didn't have much before the fire—a barber's kit, an acquaintance or two, dignity measured by the eyedropper. The Rouge disaster took everything I had.

But it gave me a chance.

The Auberge Rouge was a decrepit flophouse occupying four stories in a narrow redbrick building a block from Morningside Park. The glamorous name suggested the builder had delusions of grander boulevards than the one the Rouge actually squatted on. Maybe he had even been to Paris once. This inn was a relic of more interesting times, when World War I doughboys, cardsharps, panhandlers, rural refugees, overaged urchins, pimps, and clueless travelers had gathered in Harlem, lucky to be one step removed from the gutter.

This once-elegant street recalled a genteel era when hopeful young girls fleeing the countryside could find safe harbor in these gracious buildings. Now the block was still quiet, but the girls and men here were on the prowl, scuttling any hopes they might once have had in favor of hard transactions and easy hookups.

Broken bottles and dented cans bloomed between the cracks in the sidewalk, glinting in the moonlight from a blanket of last fall's dingy leaves. The wrought-iron fence flanking the stair leading to the inn's red door was missing many of its pickets, their delicate scrollwork mocked by the haunted neglect of the place.

The Rouge had managed to evade the attention of twenty-first-century city building inspectors through a lively application of bribes and other inducements. Some of the most effective offers were in kind: personal services arranged by Larry Sherman, the night manager. The Worm earned his nickname bartering the bodies of the tired women who were the primary occupants of the inn.

I rented a room by the month, but Patty, Colleen, and the rest of the third-floor crew rented by the night at nine dollars and fifty cents a pop.

I craved privacy more than decency, so I paid Larry the Worm twice the going rate for a double-wide cubicle with a sink hanging precariously off one wall. A six-foot-long rope stretched over the window, from which I hung my white shirts and black trousers. The suspended clothing worked as a curtain of sorts, since the original drapery had been lost years before. Swaybacked and groaning piteously, the bed sagged in the middle when I lay down, and the grimy red carpet was worn through where my feet touched each morning when I got up.

As an itinerant barber newly arrived in Harlem with a stint in the army and a busted marriage behind me, I didn't have much money to spare. The Auberge Rouge fit my budget and my mood. If that fire hadn't booted me from the Rouge, I might still be there.

At least my shoes were on when I jerked upright in bed that dawn. Being too soused to take off your pants before falling asleep had its advantages, as it turned out. Especially if a shrieking siren is going to play wake-up serenades at four thirty in the morning.

I grabbed my shirt from the ladder-back chair near the window and leaned my bare chest against the sill. Glancing west through the opening, I saw a fire engine careen around the corner and slam to a halt in front of my building. Five people of indeterminate shapes shouted at me from the street, pointing with frantic gestures toward the sky. I thought they wanted me to look up, so I did.

Over my head orange flames waved like angry banners from the windows two stories above mine. Against the dark sky, the frantic display looked like a flapping Halloween advertisement billowing out of season. I couldn't feel the fire's heat yet, perhaps because in August, Harlem's night air is no cooler than an oven anyway. Or maybe my luck was holding out one more time.

I knew there were people up there on the third floor, maybe on the fourth floor too. The old hotel was mostly empty—a hospitality center in name only. But there were a handful of regulars I was sure were still inside, girls I had spoken to only a few hours ago. Even drunk I remembered seeing them trudging up the stairs from the inn's matchbook vestibule: Colleen, Patty, and the goofy one who called herself Popsicle, and that other one with the cute pixie wig of cornflower-blue nylon. And I was pretty sure I'd stumbled past two, maybe three, men in the stairwell, their dark glances burning like skewed night lights guiding me to my room.

If any of these people were still up there, they were quiet now—dead or doped or drunk. Or perhaps they were silenced by the awesome power of the marauding fire. I could hear lots of shouting below me now but nothing from above. So I ran down rather than up—cowardly maybe, but my gut spurred me rather than my shattered courage. I could live to be braver another day.

I limped out of the smoke of the Auberge Rouge with my wallet, my pants, my shoes, and the shirt on my back. My belt, the most valuable thing I owned and a gift from my mother, was somewhere under the bed. I hoped the firefighters would soak my room with enough water so I could return in a few hours to claim it.

The shadowy gang that had signaled me from the curb had been joined by dozens of gawkers by the time I reached the street. I tried to slip into the crowd, but my exit from the Rouge drew the attention of a patrolman who called me over for an interview. This cop was slight but sinewy; his shoulders didn't quite fill out the stiff folds of his navy uniform. I couldn't make out the shape of his head or haircut with his cap pulled so low, but the face was rabbity and gaunt, distinguished by its deep-brown color and huge eyes. He hunched over a notepad as he flung questions, causing me to crouch in imitation of his stance. I told him everything I remembered, which wasn't much. During the conversation, I tried to keep my eyelids as still as possible and hoped that the smell of bourbon on my breath had been overtaken by the stink of scorched wool and burning linoleum that blanketed us.

The fire was confined to the upper two floors of the Rouge; my floor, the second, was intact, though hoses continued to drench it long after the flames receded. Watching the fight to contain the blaze provided the neighborhood with gaudy entertainment for more than two hours, the crowd growing even after the fire died. When the gaunt little cop finished with me, I retreated into the audience to wait for the third act of this drama, the one that revealed the body count. Gasps and murmurs rose from the assembly as each stretcher was paraded from the brothel's blackened carcass.

One, two...five bodies in all—just shrunken lumps under white sheets. I hated that these misshapen piles didn't dent the canvas stretchers the way real bodies should have. No arms, no protruding legs—there was nothing to assert that these were humans once. Even the exhausted firemen seemed to bear these palls lightly, as if ashes were all they could scrape from the burned-out inn to account for each soul who had perished there.

My bad foot was aching, and my back was sore from standing too long on the uneven cement. I wanted to get away from the fleshy stench and the flashing blue lights that bombarded the block at crazy angles, from the sodden grime that dripped into the gutters on both sides of the street. As the sky brightened, streaky white traces crept between the shrouded high rises to herald another hot day. But the crowd in front of the Rouge remained in night shadows.

I was torn: I wanted to escape, but I wanted to get back inside to inspect my room, salvage anything I could from its wreckage. Indecision made me teeter on the curb, and that's when the new cop caught me.

"You look like you're in a rush. Got somewhere important to be?"

I could look him in the eye, so he was six foot one, like me. He had pasty skin, stick straight black hair scraped from a harsh part, and round cheeks that pressed upward to encase his black eyes even though he wasn't smiling. Chinese probably, but other ethnicities were not ruled out. I could have fixed the haircut with a few quick scissor strokes, but the scowl seemed permanent. The suit was brown and well tailored, with a teal windowpane plaid that hinted at dandyism. His waist surpassed his chest by at least four inches. And the jacket fit too tight under the arms, like he had bought it two years ago and then got promoted to a sedentary desk job.

"So, where's the fire, pal?" I wanted to cut that smirk off his face with a straight razor.

"I've seen enough. No need to stick around." I suppressed the shrug, but I wasn't going to give him any more information than necessary.

"I understand you lived at the Auberge Rouge."

He paused and then added, "It's Rook. Shelby Rook, right?"

I wanted to correct him with the true spelling of my name: Shelba. Shelba Julio Rook. My mother, Alba Julieta, had linked her name with that of my wandering father, Sheldon, to give me a label that was both fanciful and feminine. Sheldon Rook was dark as an eclipse, smart, and *muy peligroso,* my mother told me, with a million-dollar smile and a dancer's handsome grace. But it turned out Sheldon plus Alba never added up to much besides my asphalt-gray eyes. Over the years I found out that my multiple ambiguities didn't sit well with lots of people: name, color, race, language—everything straddled one border or another. So my given name Shelba had gotten me in plenty of fights since the first day of kindergarten. No need to strike up another battle now with this cop. Shelby would do.

"Yeah, right. So, you know I already told everything to the other cop. Nothing to add."

"Well, I don't trust Nelson's note-taking abilities, so tell it to me again. When did you get home last night?"

"More like morning, around one thirty or two."

"Did you see anyone in the entrance or hallways?"

"The night manager, Larry, was at his desk, like always. And I passed two girls in the lobby."

"Which girls?"

"I saw Patty and Colleen as I crossed the lobby. They rent rooms on the third floor. They were seated in chairs and waved to me. When I got to the stairwell, I saw Popsicle too. She's from the fourth floor."

I remembered then the drawling conversation I'd had a few hours ago with the girls of the Rouge, but I didn't want to share my memories with this cop. They seemed at once too trivial and too intimate to reveal to a stranger even if the girls were no longer around to demand privacy. I could be their protector even if only in this small final matter.

———

As usual, the sallow women lounging in the tiny vestibule of the hotel hadn't let me get to the staircase without a barrage of comments.

"Long time no see, beautiful!"

"Hey, baby, I been keepin' it hot for you! Anytime, anyplace! You know you got it; just hafta ask!"

These jibes from Patty and Colleen were loud and friendly, like the lobby's ruby-red decor and gold-flocked wallpaper. And their invitations were just as fake as the acrylic on their fingertips or the squeaky leatherette on the chairs strewn around the room.

I had remained silent as always, hoping to make it to the stairs without incident.

But Patty, wearing an auburn wig this week, took up the unspoken challenge:

"Girls, any a you think the priest of the Rouge might be into threesomes?"

She had clucked and adjusted her straps so that her breasts spilled perilously close to the edge of the push-up bra.

"If you *was* into that scene, Poppy and me could work out some kinda deal. Special arrangement just for you, Fancy Face." She had pursed her lips at me and shimmied in her chair.

Out of the corner of my eye, I caught Larry the Worm behind the counter of the registration desk on the other side of the lobby. A scarred

Plexiglas barrier protected the night manager from the inhabitants of the Auberge Rouge. And vice versa. I had never seen him outside of his little cubicle, and the scratchy haze on its plastic window gave Larry a permanent dirty halo. He had rolled his eyes in the direction of Patty and leered, running a hand through the lint-colored strands of the comb-over that decorated the top of his head. My stomach had revolted at the gross gesture, urging me forward toward the stairs.

But Colleen's blue eyes had flashed then, and her country drawl warmed up the air.

"Aw, Patty, he don't want nothin' you got to give him! The man's got taste; can't you see that?"

"Taste! Mmmm, you said it!"

Popsicle pulled a long draw from her slim cigarette. With its glowing tip, she had inscribed a circle in the air around me.

"Tasteee! Mmmm, yaaas!"

She smacked her lips, and the other girls had joined in the lewd chorus, their mouths gaping and closing like painted fish.

The girls of the Rouge were a sad bunch, with their garish makeup and tawdry outfits. But even after only five weeks' residence, I knew they had my back—they were the first partners I had enlisted in my new city.

———

"Any last names for these ladies? Or any *real* names?" The cop interrupted my reverie with new prodding.

"We were only on a first-name basis. The Rouge wasn't all that friendly a place."

"That's not how I hear it. I hear it was a real cozy spot, where friends entertain friends by the hour. Like a book club or something. At least that's how Mr. Larry Sherman described it. You disagree?"

"Larry's the manager, so I take his word for it."

"The owner too, so I hear."

"I don't know about that. You'd have to check with Larry on that."

"You see anybody else before you got to your room?"

"I think I passed two men in the stairwell. Could have been three—I'm a bit cloudy on that. They continued up after I pushed through the door to the second floor."

"And these gentlemen, what did they look like? You seen them around the Rouge before last night?"

"Never seen them before. Both African American, late thirties, maybe forty. The fat one had a patch over his left eye. The other had some kind of grill or gold on his teeth."

"Nice. You caught a lot for not really noticing anything. See any tattoos, scars, identifying marks?"

"None that I saw."

"Would you have seen any more if you'd been sober?" Either he knew from Officer Nelson that I had been drunk or he could still smell the bourbon on my breath.

"Maybe. But hypotheticals aren't going to help your investigation. Or any of them either. They make it out alive?"

"Only Larry Sherman." Naturally the Worm survived.

"And you, Mr. Rook." He drew out my simple name as if the added length meant something ominous.

"So, you only knew these girls in passing—is that how I understand it? You sure about that? Nice-looking fella like yourself. You sure you didn't sample any of their offerings? I mean in a neighborly fashion, so to speak. Like borrowing sugar or something?"

"No. They weren't offering, and I wasn't borrowing, Officer." His expensive suit told me he wasn't a mere patrolman, but I wanted to needle him—even things out a bit or perhaps hurry him to end this interrogation.

"Detective." He kept his baritone smooth but squared his shoulders to remind me of my status and licked his upper lip once before continuing.

"See anything more? After you passed those two or maybe three men in the staircase?"

"Nothing. When I fell asleep, the place was quiet, and it stayed that way until the sirens woke me."

He grunted at the simplicity of my story but remained silent, which gave me an opening.

"So, what do you think caused this fire? Electrical spark? Cigarette? Leaky gas? Pipe cinders? Matches?"

"Hypotheticals don't help the investigation, do they?" Quoting my gibe back to me, he pressed his lips into a thin line that might have passed for a smile if we had been friends.

"You get any other bright ideas or you remember any more details, you can reach me here."

The card that dangled from his fat fingers was stiff, pristine, and white. It said he was "Archibald Lin, Detective. New York Police Department. Homicide Task Force." Whatever that was.

My left foot was wailing in chorus with my spine and the throbbing in my head had escalated, so I pocketed the card and used this as a farewell gesture. My pivot toward the Rouge's front door wasn't as elegant as I would have wished, but it did the trick. Lin let me go until I reached the middle of the street, when he threw his booming voice against my back.

"You limping or something? You get hurt running out of there?"

"Arthritis kicking up, Detective. That's all. I'll be fine once I get off my feet."

Not true, but he had no need to know that. An IED near Tikrit had blasted a hole in my buddy's gut and sheared off two of the toes on my left foot a few years back. The looks that swept over Bunche's face—first surprise, then acceptance, then absence—when that explosive hit still crept into my dreams every once in a while. But the hauntings were rare now, and I worked hard to keep it that way.

I didn't look back at the detective to see if my dodge had worked. Archibald Lin kept quiet after that, dropping the fake kindness, so I trudged into the soggy dimness of the Auberge Rouge in search of my few possessions.

When I explained the limited nature of my hunt, the firefighter stationed in the inn's lobby let me past the front desk. I promised to go only as far as my second-floor room after he assured me that structural damage to the building was confined to the stories above mine.

My room stank. The fire's odor was deep, like a cloud that hunched in every corner. I expected to see a sulfurous fog around my head when I looked in the mirror over the sink, but only my bloodshot eyes stared back. The smoke seemed to have clawed at my eye sockets, bruising the skin until just plum-colored shadows remained. I could measure the missed hours since my last meal in twin depressions under my cheekbones. My tongue was caked with white film, putrid and thick, and the stench of sea salt and alcohol coated my gums. I raked fingers through my hair, but the tangled curls refused to lay flat.

Crouching to look under the bed, I saw the empty bottle of Four Roses bourbon toppled on the dank rug. Next to it I found my belt coiled where I had stowed it. A single bright turquoise nugget glowed from the silver conch-shell buckle. The stone was pure, pristine blue without copper veining or freckles, the size of my pinkie nail. The damp black leather looked as though the mottling could be permanent. This belt was all I had from Alba, and I was grateful to find it intact even if stained.

I should have headed for the lobby then, but something pulled me upward. I wanted to take a look at the third floor and see for myself its burned-out ruin. There was nothing sacred about this dark corridor despite all the death it contained. The phony oriental carpet squished under my feet as I made my way to the room Colleen rented. Whether I tiptoed or plodded, the sound was organic and rude, as if I was trampling the hotel's bare flesh. The charred door hung off its hinges, canting at a zany angle. I wanted to look inside, to see where someone had died, to record a moment of respect for that lost soul. Steam in the room mixed with smoke and the remnants of her sugary cologne. A breeze pressed in through the open window, carrying the morning's humidity without freshening the space. No holy phrases rumbled through my brain then, not a single sacred word, but the ancient four-pointed gesture over my chest came automatically. I touched Alba's silver belt buckle at my waist to finish the moment of communion.

As I turned to go, I caught a flash of white metal glinting near my bum left foot. A tin rectangle was wedged between the sodden margin of the carpet and the door jamb. The shallow box might have once held matches or safety pins or a hypodermic but the enamel label on its cover was scorched beyond recognition now.

I pried open the little box, figuring that Colleen wouldn't mind the invasion anymore. Only a black business card curled inside. Its shiny surface was crowded with embossed letters in gold, green, and red: "The Ross Agency/ Private Investigations/ Lost? Missing? Cheated? Your Problems—Our Solutions." A large open eye outlined in red with lush green lashes covered most of the card. Below the eye an address was crammed into the left corner; a name, Norment Ross, Esq., squeezed into the right. The card's reverse was white, marked with only a simple inscription in a round flowing hand: "Call me whenever..." The phone number that followed this invitation began with New York City's 212 area code, but the rest was smudged and indecipherable.

I stowed the garish card in my breast pocket. With its bent edges and boastful declarations, it felt flimsy next to the sturdier cardboard Archibald Lin had given me. There was nothing either of us could do to save anybody in the Auberge Rouge now.

———

After the solitude of Morningside Park and the unyielding slats of the bench where I spent the day, the cool interior of Lonnie's Diner was a welcome refuge. When I got there, the Friday lunch crowd had mostly departed, and dinner was an hour later, so I had the undivided attention of my favorite waitress, Raye. Only a few blocks from the Auberge Rouge, Lonnie's was an easy place for a stranger to fit in. I took most breakfasts there, and when I could afford it, I splurged on dinner too.

The restaurant had seen better days, if only in the dreams of its owner. The blue-and-white checked linoleum tile floor was chipped but clean, the stuffing bursting from splits in the cushions of spinning stools along the stainless-steel counter. A crusted coffee percolator bubbled next to the rack holding menus and extra napkins near the kitchen door. Doily-covered pedestals displayed an assortment of cakes, doughnuts, and pies inside glass cabinets. Through the rectangular opening that separated the kitchen from the narrow dining room, I could see Jimi the cook's sleek head as he skated around his domain.

Slapping a laminated menu on the table in front of me, Raye didn't hold back:

"How you doing, Rook?"

She slanted her head to the right and peered closer.

"Honey, you look like the cat dragged you in, licked you over, and then left you for dead."

This was a friendly greeting, better than most Raye launched at her customers. When she wanted nothing to do with you, Raye lavished praise; when she liked you, she delivered her best jabs. Tips were not a motivation in Raye's world, and the customer was only occasionally right. Her temperament varied little, but her hairdos probed a different frontier of fashion every time I came into Lonnie's. This afternoon the style was two-toned: the back half of her head was festooned with dark-blue shingles that tapered close to the nape. The front half featured a swoop of golden bangs dangling over the left eye. I liked that her nails were lacquered navy to match her hair—and the floor tiles.

"Yeah, well this wasn't my finest day. But a cup of your coffee will sure help."

I grinned to signal I wasn't offended. But Raye leaned closer, sniffed extravagantly, and refused to let go without an explanation.

"You smell like a furnace, Rook. What's up?" The worry creasing her brow was genuine. And I knew I would never get that coffee until I had offered up the truth. My stomach rumbled, but I had to bargain a bit.

"Bring me Jimi's double burger with blue cheese, no pickles, and I'll tell you everything."

Before I could ask for it, Raye pointed me toward the restroom. I washed as best I could, twisting around in the cramped space to strip off my shirt, pumping the dispenser's green liquid soap into a foam that erased the grime from my face, neck, arms, and chest. I doused my head with cold water and hoped that the dunk under the faucet rinsed most of the smoke from my hair. Checking in the mottled mirror over the sink, I patted my cheeks with paper towels. I thought I looked decent again—a little rough around the eyes still, but acceptable.

Raye delivered the coffee, the sandwich, and a tall glass of ice water in record time. I hadn't asked for fries, but she brought those too, a rare gesture I appreciated for all the concern and care it expressed. She raked her eyes over my face, up and down my body, and then tilted her chin once. Since she didn't threaten to take me back to the restroom for a second scrubbing, I figured I passed muster.

"Now, what happened to you, Fancy Face?" I hadn't even pulled the pickle slices off the cheeseburger before Raye slid onto the bench opposite me, ready for my story.

"You know that fire at the Auberge Rouge last night?" I supposed the whole neighborhood knew about the brothel by now so I wasn't surprised when she nodded. "Well, *that* happened."

"I thought everybody in there died. Didn't hear of a single soul getting out. What was you doing up at the Rouge anyway? Don't go telling me you *pay* for that mess."

She italicized the word "pay" enough that I think she meant it as a backhanded compliment.

"I live there, Raye. Used to, anyway."

Her eyes grew glassy. "Honey, I'm sorry to hear that. You really all right?"

"Yeah, don't worry about me." Around bites of the double burger, I told Raye the story of the fire from my insider's perspective. I figured she could parlay this exclusive news to raise her status a notch or two with the senior gaggle that frequented the diner.

In return, I wanted some information too. I fished the shiny black card from my shirt and pushed it across the table toward Raye.

"I found this inside the Rouge this morning. Mean anything to you?"

Raye picked up the card and then set it down again. She took a long time pressing each corner flat before opening her mouth, so I knew she had something heavy to tell me.

"Yeah, sure, I know the Ross Agency. Old man Ross helped me out of a tight spot a few years back."

When she snapped her lips shut, I shoved the water glass over to her side, urging her to take a sip and start over.

After a moment, she did.

"A while ago, Lonnie and me, we had a bad break up. What I mean is, she ran out on me. Disappeared and left me holding the bag for the lease on our apartment and on this place too. She had skipped out on me before, so at first I wasn't worried none. But after four weeks, the bills started coming due, and I figured she had split for real this time."

A sigh ruffled the auburn fringe over her eyes, but she rolled on.

"I could always get another apartment, if it came to that. But I wanted to hang on to the diner, you know. Lonnie and me had put too much cash and too much sweat into it to give it up just that quick. So I went to Mr. Ross. Asked him to try and find Lonnie for me. Not to get her to come back to me or anything. I figured all that was over and done for. I just wanted her to cover her part of the restaurant rent and such."

Raye snatched a napkin from the stack wedged between the ketchup bottle and the pepper shaker. She dabbed at her nose and at a tear streaking toward her chin. Her eyes fixed on a point over my shoulder. I guessed that stare took in a bleak vista that was none of my business. I wanted to give her an out, a way to drop this raw story if she needed the respite, so I coughed. But then Raye seized a fry, dragged it through the pool of ketchup on my plate, and popped it in her mouth. This little theft seemed to ease the mood, and she continued, a smile curling her lips.

"And Mr. Ross, he found Lonnie for me. Never learned exactly where he went or how he did it. And I didn't ask lots a questions neither. No good ever come from asking too many questions. He found her was all I know and all I cared about. Mr. Ross got a gift for that kinda work: finding people, fixing up misery, patching together things that got torn apart. That's his specialty."

Raye's smile broadened with mischief. "So now me and Lonnie, we been back together these eight years since and never had no more trouble. Well, no more *big* trouble, I mean."

A wink thrown my way, another stolen fry, and the cloud over our table lifted.

My turn to talk again. I retrieved the business card and drew a finger over the embossed line at the bottom. I was determined to find Mr. Norment Ross. For Colleen's sake. And for my own too maybe.

"Is the Ross Agency still at this address?"

"Sure is. You know that stretch of the boulevard, dontcha?"

I nodded as Raye lined up the salt and pepper shakers and then thrust the mustard jar in the middle of the row.

"Right up in between Lee's Dry Cleaning and the Korean grocery. You'll see the Emerald Garden restaurant and the Ross Agency's right there." She tapped a navy-blue nail on the mustard jar to make her reference clear.

I angled my knees toward the edge of the bench and stood to pull out my battered wallet, but Raye waved me off.

"Ah, nah baby, no worries with that. Jimi says the cheeseburger's on the house. On account a the fire and all."

"Well, tell Jimi I appreciate it. And thanks to Lonnie too."

"Sure will. And say hey to Mr. Ross from me, will ya?"

Chapter 2
THE EMERALD GARDEN

After my second pass by the Emerald Garden Restaurant, the old boys of the whist game started chewing me over pretty good.

The store front was set back from the broad pavement, where pedestrians strolled rather than scurried by, the heat weighing them down as much as their parcels and handbags. A deep red-brick patio stretched between the restaurant's green door and the sidewalk proper. Three round white plastic tables clustered in front of the picture window, a chain snaking through their legs to prevent diners from stealing the furniture. The chipped green metal folding chairs surrounding each table were free for the taking. On each side of the patio, a line of cone-shaped bushes in cement pots formed privacy hedges shielding patrons of the Emerald Garden from Lee's Dry Cleaning to the east and the Korean grocery to the west. I knew I was at the right place because an arc of curlicued green letters across the window proclaimed the name of the restaurant.

Five men lounged around one of the tables, with no food in sight. Crumpled paper bags covering cans or bottles of refreshments cluttered the bricks next to their feet. The fierce slap of playing cards against the plastic table surface punctuated the humid air. Reverberating off the restaurant's plate glass, laughter, derisive hoots, and whistles of astonishment broke out every few seconds.

Raye's directions had seemed easy enough, but when I arrived in front of the Emerald Garden, I could find no sign of the Ross Agency. I walked by the restaurant once looking for a hidden entrance or a placard. Doubling back, I slowed my pace to make sure I hadn't missed a modest poster or at least a handwritten arrow pointing the way.

The third time I passed by, the players started in on me. Though they kept their eyes on the cards, their raised voices reached the sidewalk with ease.

"I *told* you he was coming back, Sidney. You owe me fifty cent."

"If he limps by here one more time, I'm gonna shoot him in the other leg, just to even out his snaggle-tooth walk."

"He can't be a narc, can he? Even the police knows better than to hire people look as dumb as him, don't they?"

"Hobblin'! Wobblin'! Bobblin'! You figure Junior can make it four rounds? Or is he down for the count?"

"Down goes Frazier! *Down* goes Frazier!" Snickering laughter accompanied the hands flung into the air.

The players didn't seem angry or even annoyed with me. Despite the sharpness of their words, the tone was warm, like older brothers joshing me into their circle of intimacy. The ribbing was an invitation, or at least I decided to take it like that.

I approached to within an arm's length of the table, empty palms hanging loose at my flanks. When they laid aside their cards to inspect me, I spoke up.

"Hey, fellas. How you doing? I'm just looking for an address. I must of got it mixed up or something. I'd appreciate any help you can give."

I kept my eyes trained on the scattered cards as a sign of respect, but even so I could catch a glimpse of each man.

They were all older than me by at least two decades, perhaps more. Grizzled beards, shiny scalps, leathery complexions, and knuckles bent with arthritis united them in a fraternity of dignified age. One man wore a multicolored dashiki over his undershirt, showing off thick muscles rippling beneath dark skin. Sweat gleamed on the upper lip of another, who parked a white skullcap on his equally white frizz. A rangy fellow in a green gabardine suit sported a neat goatee flecked with gray. His receding hairline was partially covered by a stingy-brimmed fedora in yellow straw. Wire-rimmed glasses fronted the blue-black face of the fourth man. The youngest of the group was also the thinnest, his chest sunken under the wool vest and long-sleeved shirt he wore despite the blazing temperature.

Sidney must have been the one in the wire-rimmed glasses because I saw him slide two quarters across the table to settle his bet with the man in the white skullcap. They grinned at each other, the brotherhood of Harlem whist players sharing a little entertainment to liven up an unremarkable summer afternoon. If I could help them pass the time this way, I was glad to be of service.

As the man in the skullcap pocketed his coins, he bent over to retrieve a slender ebony cane from between his backless slippers.

He tossed it at me, quipping, "Here, you look like you need this more than me."

He was only a yard away so the cane zipped toward me like a dart. I grabbed the stick with both hands and brought it down across my raised thigh with a swift jerk. Snapping the wooden staff made a satisfying report that echoed across the patio. That loud crack widened the eyes of every man at the card table. I didn't feel anger surging through me, certainly not fear. The adrenaline spurted because the assault was so abrupt. Performance over, I dropped the shattered halves of the cane in front of me.

"Thanks for the offer. I think I'll pass."

My audience murmured at this sudden feat, admiration tinged with anxiety I supposed, but no one spoke for another minute. Finally, the man in the dashiki turned around to face me.

"Whatchu looking for, son?" So I addressed my answer to him.

"The Ross Agency. I was told it was next to the Emerald Garden restaurant, but I can't seem to find it anywhere."

The man in the green suit threw a question in a deep voice. "What you want with the Ross Agency?"

"It's private business concerning a third party. I can't really say more than that right now." I kept my tone light but firm. I wasn't going to offer any details to this crowd.

18

All five men leaned back from the table in a single gesture. They kept their gaze on the cards fanned out in front of them, but I could detect slight twitches of brows, eyelids, and fingers as they waited. Finally, some kind of signal must have been shared; I didn't catch who gave it, but a collective breath whooshed out of them all at once.

The man in the wool vest coughed and scratched at his throat as if clearing obstructions inside and out:

"If you go into the restaurant and walk toward the back, you'll find Mei Young. She owns the place, and she can direct you to the Ross Agency."

His raspy voice caught on the last words. He coughed again before spitting out the instructions.

"Tell her you was sent by us. She'll help you out."

———

After the glare of the boulevard, the restaurant's interior felt dim and cool. I didn't smell any soy or hoisin sauce so I wondered if the Emerald Garden was really a Chinese establishment as I had assumed. The red-lacquered walls did feature embroidered images in gold frames of rampant dragons, mountains, and a pagoda-festooned garden. But the carefully hand-lettered menu posted on the opposite wall from these cliched pictures declared that the sandwiches on offer were more conventional deli fare. You could get turkey clubs, grilled cheese, jerk chicken, or two dozen varieties of subs. There were pizza by the slice and Cobb or Caesar salad too, but no fried rice, Buddha's Delight, or Moo Goo Gai Pan in sight.

The place was empty of customers, the Formica-topped tables wiped clean and bristling with silverware in anticipation of the Friday-night dinner crowd. As I stepped around the chairs, a slim figure glided forward from the shadows at the rear of the dining room. Because of the backlit bright kitchen, I couldn't tell if this silhouette was female or male.

I chanced a guess: "Hello? Mrs. Mei Young? The gentlemen outside sent me to see you."

19

She didn't offer a hand or even a smile, though a chilly bow of the head acknowledged I was on target.

Mei Young stood five feet tall and wrapped her tiny frame in white linen trousers several sizes too big. A tightly cinched drawstring of red silk kept the pants up and belted in her soft white T-shirt. With a helmet of silver hair razor-cut to complement her sharp jawline, Mei Young looked ancient and utterly modern at the same time. I saw her daily over the next six years, and this uniform varied only slightly with the seasons: black silk trousers and long-sleeved T-shirts in the winter replaced the feathery white linens of summer, accented always by the lucky red rope at her waist and a matching slash of crimson across her mouth.

In a few words, I explained my mission, and Mei Young asked no questions, simply beckoning me to follow her through the kitchen and out to the courtyard behind the building. My silent guide pointed toward an unmarked door. By the time I had twisted the handle and placed a foot on the first step of the staircase inside, Mei Young had disappeared.

———

Without carpeting, the boards of the second-floor corridor creaked under my uneven footsteps, announcing my arrival to any sentinel who cared to listen. I was glad to see that at last, in this dusty passage, the Ross Agency was prominently advertised. The frosted glass of the door at the end of the hallway was blazed with the firm's name in gold letters three inches high. Below them was an eye outlined in bold red strokes with flaring green lashes, a giant match for the image on the business card that had brought me here. I knocked on the glass and invited myself into the office without waiting for a response.

I didn't know what Norment Ross looked like, but I was positive that the gorgeous woman stretched out before me was not him. The nameplate on her desk said, "Sabrina Ross," so I guessed she might be related.

She was tipped back in an old-fashioned swivel chair, her bare feet crossed and planted on the corner of the wooden desk that crowded the small reception area. At that angle, it was hard to miss that her naked feet were connected to equally bare caramel brown legs that ended, after a long well-sculpted journey, in the disappointment of frayed blue jean shorts.

A peasant blouse tipped by blue flowers along the shoulders disguised the rest of her figure. But the dangling tassels at her throat promised that when she moved, more loveliness would surely be revealed. Her right hand disappeared into a black cloud of hair, holding a phone to her hidden ear, I assumed. That hair celebrated a life all its own, a festival of billowing coils and shimmying mass that cascaded over her collarbones and partied down her back.

A heart-shaped face, smooth and sweet, punctuated by big brown eyes and a wide mouth completed the picture. I didn't like the black lipstick, but I could work around that. Poetry had never been my strength, but as the silence extended, I started to search for fancier words to describe her beauty. Six years later, I'm still searching.

She hadn't missed my entrance; I was sure of that. She was stationed right in front of the door, making it hard to overlook me. And she was staring straight at me, so I knew her silence was intentional. Whether to assess me, rattle me, strip me of every defense, whatever her purpose, it was working. She kept quiet for many seconds, until I could feel the tops of my ears start to tingle, a sure sign that a flush was rising along the back of my neck. Dusky-red ears revealing emotional intensity was a trait I had inherited from fair-skinned Alba—an exposure I would have gladly traded away in that moment.

"Pinky, hold up a minute. Let me get back to you. Yeah, see you in a while."

The voice was strong, not girlish but mellow and deeper than her baby face suggested. She put down the phone next to a closed laptop and swung her feet to the floor. As she leaned forward on the desk, her scent drifted to me: vanilla undercut with something intoxicating like amber and fig or another dark fruit.

"Can I help you?"

I couldn't answer except with the plain truth:

"Yes. Yes, you can."

When I didn't say anything further, she cocked her head to one side and let a smile quirk her lips. She seemed almost tender then, but no pity or scorn curled her mouth, just acceptance of my unvarnished honesty and need.

"Well…?"

I pulled out the business card from my shirt pocket and held it in the air between us.

"I'm looking for Mr. Norment Ross. Is he in?"

"No, I'm afraid you missed him. Can I take a message?"

She made no attempt to round up a pen or paper, continuing to challenge me with her frank stare. I felt as though she could see each singed fiber and scorched stain on my collar. I was sure she could smell the smoke still clinging to my shirt and skin. I looked down to check the black line of grime that circled each nail.

To deflect her attention, I asked about the agency. If I could get her talking, I could keep her from wondering about my ramshackle appearance.

"Does the Ross Agency take clients off the street?"

"We take on all kinds of customers—walk-ins and references too. Our business is security. You come to us if you need protection for your family, or you want guards at your party, or you had a break-in at your office, or you just need a little mystery solved. We investigate problems the police are too snooty or too hassled to take on."

She paused the recitation of this mission statement to see if she was on the right track with me.

"You need something investigated? You lost someone? Lots of people go missing in Harlem. We find the ones who want to be found. The rest, well, they stay lost. You looking for somebody? We can help you with that."

"That's OK. I really wanted to speak directly with Mr. Ross. I'll come back another time. When do you expect him to return?"

Her eyes glanced away then, skipping from my face to focus over my left shoulder. I thought she was trying to hide her distaste at my appearance, but I was wrong.

"Right about *now*, junior!"

The jovial voice boomed in my ear, rich with good humor. Norment Ross looked delighted that I jumped an inch in the air as the girl laughed out loud. The whist player in the green suit loomed over me, his fedora pushed back at a precarious angle, his dark face split by a grin that encompassed a continent's worth of gleaming teeth. The white bristles of his goatee complemented the pristine ivory of his eyes, and the temperature in the room seemed to rise several degrees as he exhaled in glee.

"Gotcha good, didn't I?" Ross winked at me, as if I was in on the joke from the start. He clapped a massive hand on my shoulder and squeezed until I winced.

Shouting, he formalized my introduction:

"Brina, you should have seen how he took Rashid's cane and broke it across his knee with one blow. Never seen anything like it. Mighty impressive, junior, mighty impressive. You got to go a long way to impress me, but that was a good one."

Brina didn't seem quite as moved by my stunt as Ross was; skepticism chased disdain across her face, and her pretty mouth turned down slightly. I felt she was working hard to resist rolling her eyes.

"Daddy, he has one of your business cards. Somebody must have referred him to us."

Still grinning, Ross extended his hand to me, wriggling his fingers. "Let's have a look here."

Ross sobered as he scanned the inscription on the reverse of the card. It was as though a sudden thundercloud had dropped around his ears, pressing vertical lines between his eyes and creasing his brow.

"Where'd you get this, mister…?"

"My name's Rook. And I got it at the Auberge Rouge. Last night, after the fire."

"Did Colleen give it to you?" His voice, softening to a whisper now, caught over the lost girl's name.

"No, she didn't make it out, I'm afraid. I found the card in her room after the firemen were done."

Sorrow replaced mirth on Ross's face as he took in the news. Brina looked puzzled by the grim weight that had descended onto her father, so I let her take the lead in questioning. If the sentiments were raw, it wasn't my business to pry, even though I was eager to learn more.

"Did you know her, Dad? Was she a friend? Or a client?"

"Yeah, I knew her—sweet little girl from South Carolina, like me. Well, not *like* me, of course. But still we struck up a home feeling all the same."

Ross dragged the hat off his head, crushed it against his chest, and turned abruptly, retreating toward the back of the office suite. Over his head he waved a beckoning hand.

"Sabrina, come on back here. I need to sit down on this one."

Brina clutched my elbow, and I let her steer me to her father's private office.

When we got there, Ross was already seated behind a large old-fashioned banker's desk, and he gestured at two leather club chairs squatting in the middle of the room. Faint fumes of Old Spice aftershave wafted from the blotter on Ross's desk, conveying ease along with a touch of tradition. Brina and I dropped into the chairs. We didn't say a word, letting the old man resume his story.

"Colleen McClatchy was her name. I don't figure she was more than nineteen, if that. She came up here two years ago from a little chicken-scratch town called Piney Mount. I'm from Charleston, but I been through Piney Mount a few times. So when she came around, we hit it off—had something to talk about, laugh about right from the start. Colleen was a feisty little thing, flashing those blue eyes like Fourth of July sparklers. She said right off she didn't want my help with the meth habit. And she already had found a means to pay her way in the city. I tried to warn her, but she wasn't about to listen to an old man like me. All she wanted was for me to scare off this john who had got too involved. He got hung up on her, she said. Stuck on her like ugly on a ape."

Here Ross smiled—no teeth but a slight upward tug on his lips. He drew a large white handkerchief from the inside pocket of his suit jacket.

He wiped the cloth over his entire face twice as if drawing a curtain for a moment's privacy. Then he continued Colleen's story.

"This bully was bad for business, was how she saw it. Driving her other johns away. So, I visited with the man a few times, suggested he push off, leave Colleen alone. May have roughed him up a bit in the course of our conversations, but no one got hurt. Not seriously anyway. And he did stay away, far as I could tell. Anyway, Colleen never complained about a return visit or nothing. And I spoke with Larry Sherman, you know, the night manager at the Rouge. I told Larry to keep a look out for Colleen's bully too. Never heard from Larry neither, so I figure everything was copasetic. I gave Colleen my card and told her to call me if ever she needed my help. But I never heard from her again from that day to this."

Ross sighed through pursed lips and again passed the handkerchief over his face to remove the shine and the tears. Shaking his heavy head, he repeated his epitaph for Colleen:

"Sweet little girl from South Carolina, like me."

Brina lowered her eyes to study a crack in the arm of her leather chair. Not out of shame at witnessing her father weep, I thought, but to give him another moment of privacy. I did the same. Norment Ross was a detective—tough, shrewd, and seasoned. But hard boiled didn't apply.

———

When Ross rejoined us after a short escape to the bathroom at the other end of the office suite, his mood had lifted. He hooked the green jacket on a coat-tree behind the door and rolled up the sleeves of his yellow dress shirt, with deliberate care, as if ready for business. Droplets of water twinkled from his beard and eyelashes as he sat on the front edge of the desk, looming over me and his daughter.

"And what did you say you do for a living, Mr. Rook?" Large teeth flashing at me looked almost predatory.

"I didn't...exactly." As I squirmed to avoid Ross's gaze, the ancient leather creaked under my weight.

"I trained as a barber. But I guess you could say I'm between opportunities right now." I hoped that sounded jaunty rather than pathetic.

"Good. Good. Glad to hear it. 'Cause I've got your first assignment for you right here." The boom was back in his voice; the spark returned to his eye.

"I need you to escort Brina this afternoon. She carries deposits to the bank every Friday, and it's just about closing time."

She opened her mouth to object to this arrangement, but Ross continued talking, raising his voice a bit to show he was handing out orders, not bargaining.

"I don't know how much she got in that envelope—Brina's the brains and the bean counter of the outfit, if you haven't figured that out by now. But it's enough so I want a little extra protection for her on the walk to the bank today. Four blocks won't tax your leg too much, will it, Mr. Rook?"

"I can make it just fine. When do we start?"

———

With Brina by my side, a backpack containing the cash slung over her shoulder, those four blocks flew by in a thrilling blur.

We passed missionaries with pamphlets piled on folding tables jostling for precious space with salespeople hawking knock-off purses. Scabby-kneed cherubs zoomed past chocolate nymphs, their belly buttons winking above low-riding jeans. Office girls sweating through their polyester blouses brushed against sharp-suited matrons armored with stacks of cowrie shell bracelets. Old women with crumpled faces pushed baby carriages as they quarreled with equally ancient men fastened to their elbows. Ballers and tycoons, snitches and deacons, busboys and truckers, instigators and soothsayers—everybody was hustling to punch that invisible clock.

Despite the heat, the boulevard seemed energized, pulsing with sensuous anticipation, people driving for an unseen goal that lit their faces and turned their feet into pistons. Maybe what I sensed buzzing through the crowd was just the exhilaration of the weekend coming or the relief of an unfettered Friday night. Maybe having a job to do and a pretty girl to do it with was enough to infect me with the excitement coursing through that throng. Whatever it was, their viral high inflamed me.

The challenge of navigating that chockablock bustle prevented us from talking much, which was more than all right with me. I would have gladly walked another hour or two with Brina if I could have figured out a way to delay completing this assignment. As it was, we got to the entrance of the People's First Bank of Harlem at three minutes past six, and only a beguiling look from Brina persuaded the guard to let us in the locked door.

All that energy boiling over in the street seemed to evaporate inside the bank's chilly lobby. Everybody moved at a slug's pace between the fog-gray marble pillars. I wondered why Brina chose to join the longest of the two lines creeping toward the counter; maybe she wasn't in a hurry to end our task either. When we reached the head of the line, Brina's reason became clear: the teller, a bright-faced woman with a short ginger Afro and a gap between her front teeth, broke into a grin at our approach.

"Brina, girl, I thought sure you weren't going to make it tonight! What happened to you?"

The woman flashed her copper-colored eyes at me. I shrugged to convey a world of innocence and shoved my hands in my pockets to hide the dirty nails. If this was Brina's friend, no need to tank the first impression.

"Don't worry about him, Pinky. He's a new hire, just tagging along to get the hang of how we do things at the Agency." I was thrilled to hear this. Only a soldier's pride kept me from sinking to the marble floor in relief.

Pinky scrunched up her nose, compressing the confetti of rosy-brown freckles that sifted across her pale face. She sized up the situation in a few withering words:

"New muscle, huh? Hope he lasts."

"Ah, come on, Pinky; don't be like that. He's all right." Brina reached inside her backpack and fished out an envelope stuffed with cash. As she emptied the money on the counter and shoved it toward her friend, she offered a proper introduction.

"Pinky, this is Rook." She didn't know my first name yet, so she had to stop there.

"And Rook, this is Dieudonne Michel. Don't let her sour face fool you. In a tight fix, Pinky is the one you want with you."

"Glad to meet you, Miss Michel."

"Manners *and* a drawl? Where'd you drop in from, honey? Outer space?"

"San Marcos, Texas. About halfway between San Antonio and Austin."

That news was enough to silence both women for a full minute. Brina slanted her eyes to watch me without a direct stare. Pinky glued her gaze to the counter's slick surface. The teller completed counting the bills, registered the deposit, and printed out the receipt before uttering a follow-on comment.

"Well, Brina, that's three thousand one hundred seventy-five. That how you make it?"

Agreeing with the count, Brina stashed the receipt in the embroidered back pocket of her shorts.

We were the final customers in her line, so Pinky had some time. She leaned closer to whisper an invitation.

"If you come by the club this weekend, you can bring him. If you want that is."

She raised her chin in my direction, which I took as an endorsement, the best I could hope for on short notice.

"Yeah, well we'll see, Pinky. No telling what'll turn up between now and then, is there?"

I didn't like the casual dismissal of this opportunity, but Brina's reserve held firm, and I was hardly in a position to push.

Back on the sweltering street, Brina explained the invitation.

"Pinky only does this bank teller thing as a side gig. To make ends meet, you know. Her real job is she's a singer. Blues, jazz, whatever. Half the stuff she sings, I've never heard before. But she's got an amazing voice.

Blows the top of your head off one minute and knifes your heart the next. She's amazing. Anyway, Pinky works at a club called Jumeaux. Owned by two brothers, the Dreyfus twins."

She paused to let his new information sink in.

"Jew-mow? What's that supposed to mean?" I exaggerated the pronunciation even though I had an idea of the definition.

"Jumeaux is French for twins. See, the Dreyfus brothers named the place after themselves. They're Haitians, like Pinky."

"She sounded American like you or me."

"Oh, she is. Only her parents came from Haiti. Pinky was born right here in Harlem. Same with the Dreyfus boys."

As we strolled back to the Emerald Garden, steamy night breezes lifted Brina's hair from her brow and blew plumes of her amber scent toward me. The tickling gusts caused smiles to chase across her golden face. Talk drifted out of me: fire and brothels, family and weird mash-up names, turquoise nuggets and missing toes. Sentences and paragraphs floated from me that evening—more than I'd shared with anyone in a long time. But I didn't want Brina to think my entire life was one jagged saga of misery. So I made her shudder at my mock recipes for armadillo enchiladas and possum tacos. Then I described a Hill Country cousin whose tongue was so long he could lick his eyelid with its tip. These tall tales brought out her throaty laugh and set the tassels of her peasant blouse dancing across her breast. I wanted more of all that.

Norment Ross and Mei Young were seated opposite each other at the back of the restaurant when we arrived. Two empty salad bowls and two longneck bottles of beer stood sweating on the square table, a companionable silence separating them from the raucous diners toward the front of the room. They looked like a couple, although I knew it was foolish to jump to conclusions so quickly. Maybe Norment was a ladies' man, and casual flirtation was the currency of his everyday interactions. Perhaps the icy Mei Young unbent for everyone who wasn't a complete stranger. But something in the easy way Ross's ankles grazed the legs of the table next to Mei's slippers made me feel my speculation wasn't farfetched.

Since he hadn't waved us both over to the table, I stood in the kitchen entrance while Brina consulted with her father. I didn't know if I was discharged, if my first assignment was successful, or if I'd been a bust. Our silent passage upstairs to the Ross Agency suite convinced me I was dismissed, an impression reinforced when Brina counted out crisp bills from her wallet. As she slipped the money into a letter-sized envelope, I felt certain this was severance pay.

But then she marched me into a small office I had not seen before. The furniture resembled that in Ross's office—an old-fashioned desk, a secondhand rolling library chair behind it, and a row of metal filing cabinets against the back wall. But this set up had a welcome innovation: a plump leather couch more than seven feet long faced the desk.

"Daddy says you can stay here if you want. Just until you get yourself settled in a new place, you know. If you want."

I wanted. Very much.

"Thank you, yes. This looks perfect. I'll be out of your hair as soon as I can. I appreciate it."

I was burbling so I clamped my idiot mouth shut and just let my grin do the rest of the talking. My knees turned liquid just then and livid spots swam before my eyes. This long day was catching up to me at last. I sagged onto the couch an instant before I would have tumbled to the floor.

Brina laid the envelope with my pay on the desk. She set a small stack of business cards on the desk and then left the room, closing the door behind her. I stretched out on the sofa, holding a Ross Agency card at arm's length over my head. My arms trembled with this trivial effort, and I felt woozy.

The garish crimson eye with its extravagant green lashes seemed to wink at me once, twice, and then again. I looked for Norment Ross's name next to the agency's address on the slick black surface, but the space was blank. I exhaled with the realization: these cards were meant for me.

I was sure Brina had me read from the outset. I still couldn't figure out why she didn't say no to me the moment we met. Sullen as any other Iraq veteran, I blamed the two missing toes for the way that things of value always seemed to skip just out of my grasp. Couldn't possibly be the surly temper since I stifled that little flaw pretty well. Or the sour mouth because I zipped my lip most of the time. Brina had to have seen all of that in me from the start. And yet she agreed when Old Man Ross decided to give me a trial at the Agency.

I puzzled over this, wondering why the river of luck had turned for me. I couldn't figure it out right then; maybe it would come to me in the morning or the morning after that. With a somber rush, sleep pressed down on my chest then, its dense soft blanket swaddling my head in warmth.

Chapter 3
THE SILVER ARTICULATED FISH EARRINGS

The next weeks were crammed with cases small and smaller. Detection blended with prying; investigation seemed like gossip more often than not. Though I was occupied with new work, the fire at the Auberge Rouge never flickered out entirely. When busy days on the streets dwindled into quiet evenings back in my office, plumping a pillow for the couch or draping freshly washed shorts on the file cabinets, images of flaming banners sometimes burst over me. My scalp pumped out waves of heat, and the soles of my feet burned until I rocked back on my heels. I rushed to open a window, gasping for a cool breeze. I swallowed those burned remains of the Rouge as best I could, pushing on into new assignments, grateful for the distraction no matter how trivial the work seemed.

On day two on the job, I discovered that Brina carried a small-caliber revolver, usually strapped next to her breast in a brown leather holster and sometimes secured in her jeans waistband at the hollow of her back. I hadn't come across any opportunities for her to use the weapon, but I assumed she wouldn't do so on a mere whim. I wondered if her father also owned a gun, but I prized the job more than I honored my curiosity, so I kept these questions to myself. After a few days, I learned that Wednesdays were father-and-daughter time at the shooting range, a date they rarely missed. Shortly after that Ross told me that he and Brina both had private-investigator licenses and that their status allowed me to operate under their direction. I soon realized that the Ross Agency was the fix-it bureau for the neighborhood: challenges were never too minor to capture Norment Ross's compassionate attention. Or too repetitive to earn his disdain. Brina claimed our business was security, not therapy. But by the end of the first month on the job, I wasn't so sure.

The second time I returned Mrs. Carla Abernathy's yellow tomcat Peaches to her loving embrace, I complained to Brina about the assignment. I tried to keep my tone light to not challenge her authority, but I did feel I could share my judgment, at least in this little matter.

"You know, that cat wasn't really lost; he was shacking up with another family. Living the high life two blocks away from Mrs. Abernathy's apartment building. That's where I caught him, soaking up the sun on the back stairwell. Fat, happy, polishing his yellow ears like he owned the place."

I was leaning over her desk, two fists pressed into the wood on either side of the nameplate. Brina was draped over her chair, swiveling back and forth as we talked. She had on a navy T-shirt with pink paisley designs dancing on it, ice-blue faded jeans, two rows of heavy amber beads around her neck, and two more amber nuggets bobbing below her mane of coiling hair. She looked like a college sophomore, although I had pried out of her that she was in fact thirty-five years old.

"Aww, Rook, say it ain't so!" Brina's drawl was delicious, and her lopsided grin squeezed my heart. "Don't tell me that sweet little old Peaches is a bigamist?"

"A *trig*-amist, actually. That was the second apartment building I found him at in eleven days."

I remembered Brina's words from the first day we'd met: Lots of people go missing in Harlem. We find the ones who want to be found. The rest, well, they stay lost. I wondered if she would argue that this pessimistic observation applied to cats too.

"Not that you're counting or anything, hmmm?"

"It's his natural impulse. It's what cats do." I shrugged to show I wasn't being a scold—only philosophical. No judgment but a good dollop of cynicism.

But Brina's response pulled me up short: "So Peaches is sort of like Mrs. Abernathy's long-gone husband, you figure?"

I felt sheepish and mean then, unable to offer even a threadbare defense of my sex. "I didn't know about her husband."

"Well, Mrs. Abernathy wouldn't just go and share all that with you, now would she? Most of us around the neighborhood remember back when Harold played her for a fool. Like he thought he was smart. And she was blind, deaf, and dumb. Almost two years of cheating before she finally called him out and kicked his sorry ass to the curb. She brought home Peaches a few months after Harold packed his bags. And that cat's been with her ever since."

I stood back a little, not knowing what to say to these revelations. I felt clumsy and awkward at this new game of healing by detection. But Brina seemed a patient teacher, and her next words soothed me.

"Anyway, Mrs. Abernathy said you were tremendous, treated her and Peaches with such care. 'Tender respect' was how she put it. I liked that, Rook. You made us look good."

Platitudes came to mind, so I spouted one: "Customer's always right, I guess. Even if the customer is a tomcat's sugar mama."

"You better believe it!" Chuckling, Brina picked up a file folder and spread it on the desk.

"Not only that, satisfied customers bring us new business. Like Mrs. Abernathy here. We have a new assignment thanks to her recommendation. Who knew she was connected with the high-flying artsy-fartsy crowd? I just thought she was a school librarian."

In a few colorful paragraphs, Brina outlined our next job.

At only forty years old, Sebastian Nestor had already reeled in two Tony awards for his inventive music. Critics said these were uncomfortable compositions that forced jangling dissonance to play nice with scratchy hooks and tunes no one could hum. Fawning fans said he was cool. His Danish wife, Annemarie, was a gifted dancer and choreographer, currently on a break to raise the couple's three children. Looking for space to encompass their young family and the two studios their artistic work required, the Nestors had discovered a huge brownstone on Striver's Row in Harlem. Renovation of this ramshackle pile had consumed two years and over two million dollars. Now complete, the Nestors arrived in June and by October were ready to invite their downtown friends, colleagues, and financial angels to an uptown house warming to celebrate their good fortune and spanking new home. The party was to be extravagant: invitees glittering, decor audacious, and the Harlem-sourced caterers renowned.

Though Sebastian Nestor styled himself as a man of the people, the party was exclusive. So the Nestors had asked their new neighbor Carla Abernathy for a suggestion, and based on her enthusiastic recommendation, they engaged the Ross Agency to provide discreet security for the event. Brina and I were to screen guests at the door, checking names against a vast list, keeping out the uncouth, the unwashed, the unknown, or the blatantly stoned.

———

The evening of the Nestor party, I cooled my heels at a table in the Emerald Garden, waiting for Brina to pick me up.

With my second envelope of cash, I'd bought three pairs of pants: two black and one ink blue. They were cheap, but they did the job. I also bought four dress shirts: two white and two black, and two polo-neck shirts in light blue. So my clothing combinations were far from infinite, and I was going to have to save up for an overcoat before the weather turned. For this event, I chose to go with all black, a nod to the theatre crowd's preferred color scheme. I thought that Alba's silver belt set off the outfit with a bit of dash.

I wasn't quite daydreaming, but a pot of Mei Young's tea had failed to perk me up, so I was caught by surprise when Detective Archibald Lin dropped into the chair opposite me. He looked the same as when I had first met him outside the smoldering Auberge Rouge: the same tight suit and the same tight smirk. I didn't like him any better on second viewing.

"You cleaned up good, Rook. Honest living will do wonders for a man, won't it?"

I had no patience for the small talk and phony empathy the cop was offering.

"How'd you find me here, Detective Lin? Bamboo telegraph?"

Inside I flinched. The cliché sounded corny, maybe slightly racist. But I couldn't find out if Lin was sensitive until I pushed, so I let the insult ride.

He laughed, his mouth a round dark hole in his face, and pointed a finger at me. "Good one, Rook. In fact, you're sort of right."

Lin shifted the direction of his index finger from my nose toward the rear of the restaurant. When I twisted around, I saw Mei Young perched at her usual seat in the back. Without a smile, she nodded twice, first at Lin and then at me.

"I grew up around here. My aunt worked at Lee's Dry Cleaners next door, and my uncle cooked here at the Emerald back when it actually *was* a Chinese restaurant. My mother used to leave me here every Saturday while she cleaned office buildings downtown. So you see, this block was my playground, and Mei Young was my babysitter. Sort of my stand-in aunt. She is one tough fortune cookie. I can't tell you how many times she rescued me from fights with the grocer's kid next door."

A fleeting scowl crossed the detective's flat face. It was hard to imagine the refrigerator-size Archibald Lin as a scrawny kid, but I guess cops could be victims of bullies too.

"So when Auntie Mei told me you were camped out at the Ross Agency, I decided to stop by for a chat, welcome you to the neighborhood and all."

His smile did seem neighborly almost. But then a harder glint pierced his gaze. He leaned forward, both pudgy hands spread on the table between us.

"And I wanted to pick your brain about the Rouge fire. I'm following up on a few leads, most of them circling right back to Larry Sherman. Do you think he could be good for the fire?"

"I don't know, Lin; you're the detective. I've thought a lot about it, but I can't come up with anything except unlucky accident. Do you have evidence that says otherwise?"

Lin seemed eager to share his findings, and he dived into the details with gusto.

"Right off fire-department inspectors were suspicious about a blaze that started on the third floor and spread upward. They said it doesn't usually happen that way. It looked deliberately set to them. Then the insurance boys got wind of the inspectors' doubts and added a few of their own. They said their research showed that Sherman was underwater with the mortgage. The building was costing him much more than it was worth. He'd tried to sell it a few times in the past three years, but nobody was willing to take on the expense of fixing it up to meet code as a hotel. It was too big to be a private residence. And too poorly designed to turn into upscale condos. That block is so run-down even the most brazen cowboy developers steered clear. So your pal Larry the Worm was stuck with a stinking, rat-infested white elephant. It turns out that fire brought him a world of good luck just in the nick of time."

I had nothing more to add. "Sounds about right to me. Clear, straight-forward case of arson. Pointing right at Larry. So when're you going to arrest him?"

The detective leaned back in his chair, torturing the furniture until it groaned.

"As soon as I track him down. The Worm has gone to ground, so to speak. Nelson is working with me on this case, and we been searching for Sherman all these weeks now. Turned up nothing. Zilch, zip, nada." Lin popped his lips to emphasize the futility of police efforts in this case.

The penny dropped at last. "So you're hoping I'll do a little digging for you. Is that it, Lin?"

"Sure, why not? You got eyes and ears in the neighborhood, don'tcha? And Boss Ross and his little girl can help out too. Why not?"

"Why not is because the Ross Agency is a business, not a charity. If you're not paying, I doubt Ross will take on police work out of the goodness of his heart."

I liked seeing Lin squirm at that reprimand. He seemed a little sick, which was a good look on him. But then I relented.

"On the other hand, I might just want to give you a boost." Lin's eyes cracked open with renewed hope. A look I liked even better.

"Yeah, see Larry Sherman owes me money. I paid a security deposit of one month's rent and another month's rent in advance before I moved into the Rouge. The security deposit was supposed to cover any damages I might inflict on the place during my stay."

At that irony, I laughed without showing my teeth, and Lin nodded in fellow feeling. We were getting to the same page pretty rapidly.

"So I figure the Worm owes me six hundred dollars. If I find him first, I guess you won't mind if I shake him for the cash before I turn him over to the police?"

"Be my guest. Just leave him in one piece so we can pin the arson rap on him."

"Will do."

With our pact sealed by his sparkling eyes and genuine smile, Lin turned expansive, giving me an insider's look at his daily lot in life.

"My lieutenant's getting antsy to solve this one. He's crawling up my ass because these community agitators are stirring up trouble for the department. Do-gooders crying about how we're slow-walking the Rouge fire investigation because all that got killed was a bunch of hookers and a few johns. They're whining like the fire was some kind of gentrification move to clean up the neighborhood. We want to close this case. Proving it's arson and pinning it on Sherman will work out just fine for everybody."

Except Larry the Worm, I thought. But he had no standing in this discussion, so he was easy to ignore. I extended my hand over the table, and Lin shook it with vigor.

"When you run him down, just call me with the address. If I'm not in, leave a message for me or Nelson. We'll take care of the rest. This works out, Rook, I'll be in your debt."

Obligation, connection, even a tentative alliance. I liked the sound of that. A lot.

———

Brina pulled up a few minutes after Archibald Liu departed. Her idea of fancy dress leaned toward a variation on her bohemian look: over a pair of skinny black jeans, she wore a long loose white caftan frosted with heavy silver embroidery along the neck. The embroidery spread like a metallic web down the caftan's open sides, shivering as she walked. A spoiler undershirt blocked the view, but she still looked amazing. She bound her hair with a wide snowy wrapper, which gathered the curls into a high crown. She had wiped the usual black lacquer from her lips, and they shimmered under clear gloss.

Dangling beside her face were fantastical fish earrings in a lightweight silver that glittered in the restaurant's fluorescent glare. As she moved before me, articulated segments hinged with delicate pins made the jewelry flutter and shimmy in imitation of its watery inspiration. The fins of each section were etched in wavy black lines that added to the illusion. The metal fish were mismatched; one earring had eyes made of tiny red glass, and the other had two specks of turquoise instead. They were beautiful, regal, and long enough to graze her collar bone when she walked. Brina looked beautiful, like a mermaid princess gracing dry land just for me.

Overcome, I couldn't say anything until we reached her car, but then the emotion spurted out in a single burst:

"Those silver fish earrings are just like ones my grandmother used to wear when I was a little boy. They're amazing. They really take me back. They're beautiful on you, Brina; so beautiful."

Brina smiled at the compliment, the first I'd given her. When she said nothing, I clamped my mouth shut to avoid sounding silly or shallow, as if her physical attributes were all I cared about.

As she steered the car, shadows cloaked her face so that only the silver earrings caught the lamplight. The effect was subtle, uncanny. Darkness made it easier for me to answer her questions about Alba's family.

"My mother said that my great-grandmother Julia brought the silver articulated fish earrings with her to Texas when she and my great-grandfather fled the Mexican revolution. She passed them down to my grandmother Julieta when she died, and every time my mother brought me for a visit, Julieta had them on. The fish had turquoise eyes like your right one does. And the tarnish made the earrings look smoky black against her neck."

Memories flooded over me, drowning the words in my mouth. I remembered my grandmother calling me her poor *Negrito*, her dear *Ninito*. She never called me Shelba; perhaps she rejected that name because it reminded her that my father was inextricably linked to my mother through me. But I thought she loved me all the same. I remembered the powdery scent of Julieta's deep bosom and the rose oil she used to plait her waist-length black braids. *Pobrecito Negrito*.

I paused to study Brina's profile. Her eyes were fixed on the road, but she hummed a note of encouragement to show she was listening. I wanted her to know this, to know me in this way, so I continued once I had regained my voice.

"Those earrings must be among my earliest memories, from when I was two, maybe three. At first, of course, I didn't understand what they were. I thought my grandmother Julieta was a witch who had cast a spell on live fish and made them dangle from her ears by magic. The way they danced and jumped as she talked reinforced my belief. She was a witch—a good witch—but still a witch. And my grandmother, being the mischievous woman that she was, didn't bother to tell me the truth. I guess I must have believed in that enchantment until I was eight years old, maybe more. I can't ever remember *abuelita* Julieta without those silver fish earrings."

Sudden tears clogged my throat, and I was glad for the darkness that covered them. We found a parking spot a few doors from our destination. The stillness in the car spooked me, but when I turned back to Brina, she nodded at me, a light smile playing across her lips.

"When Julieta died, my mother decided those magical earrings should go to the grave with her. So from that day to this, I haven't seen another pair like it. I guess that's why I was so stunned when I saw you wearing them just now."

"Is that why, Rook?"

Leaning sideways, Brina turned her eyes on me then, and I felt the air between us ripple like seawater. I wanted to kiss her, and she wanted to kiss me. Her hand grazed my chin, and I pressed my lips over hers, the touch dry, the contact light and fleeting. When our mouths separated, I didn't pull back, but set my forehead to hers, breathing deeply.

"We're here." She said the simple phrase without guile, but I caught its double meaning and echoed her. "Yes, we are. Wherever that is. We're here."

———

The Nestor housewarming fulfilled every extravagant expectation anyone had had for the evening.

The interior of the four-story house was coated in white paint from ceiling to floor, showcasing the stark modern furnishings like gems in a gallery display. Tall windows bowed to the street behind ivory drapes, staircases rose encased in carved aluminum panels, and marble and polished concrete sheathed everything that wasn't made of stainless steel or glass. In contrast to all the white and cream, leather and silk, a black Steinway piano stood alone in a niche near the front parlor's picture window.

If I hadn't already been Sabrina-dazzled before I walked up the limestone steps, I would have been blinded by the sight that met me inside the place. Everything at this party was sleek, white, and expensive—including the guests.

Brina and I set up our screening operation at a table just beyond the front door inside the double-height vestibule. We kept the visitor line moving but made sure to check off each name against the list Sebastian Nestor had provided. Ignoring us as mere hired help, guests stalked past like wax figures come to life. I recognized a few of the A-listers from glossy magazines in the barber shop. But Brina was better at the name game. She whispered thumbnail sketches of the celebrities who cooed and power-kissed their way from parlor to dining room to kitchen and back. Self-congratulation propelled the circuit, but I was sure a heavy dose of envy salted the path. I looked for Mrs. Carla Abernathy's name on the guest list but didn't find it. Maybe the librarian was on a Mediterranean cruise and couldn't make it back in time. Or maybe, just maybe, the Nestors had neglected to invite their neighbor to the party.

I paid particular attention to our hosts. Sebastian Nestor was thin and gangly, with a pencil neck that seemed too fragile to support his huge head of black ringlets. Although it wasn't directed at me, I recognized that pure animal charisma radiated from him in commanding waves. If all the pink cheeks and trembling eyelids were any indication, he set most female hearts fluttering wherever his gaze landed. Nestor was an alpha male surveying his entourage, and he made sure the rest of us understood our place in the pride. His black turtleneck and narrow slacks seemed overly confining for these still-warm days of October, but I guessed the sweater's plush cashmere made up for any discomfort. Sebastian Nestor was alluring, and Brina's moist lips and eyes indicated that even she was taken with his charm. He could have any woman in the place. I wondered how many of the guests here had enjoyed his charisma up close.

So I found it curious that the only woman in the room who seemed impervious to his appeal was his own wife, Annemarie. She too was thin and tall but carried herself with the coiled grace her husband lacked. She was not beautiful by any conventional standards, but she was arresting. You couldn't take your eyes from her when she decided to turn up her star power. Her icy blondness was enhanced by a sleeveless steel-gray top and matching pants that swept the floor. I never got a glimpse of the three children; Annemarie said they were upstairs in the nursery with a nanny, but I assumed that the offspring of this glittering couple were as gorgeous as the parents.

As the invitees filed in, Annemarie stood near her husband but apart, as if a glass wall separated them. They seemed not to see each other, even as they basked in the admiration of their guests. Sebastian seemed unaffected by the balletic glamour of his wife. He scanned the room with a searching gaze that seemed to pin everything and everyone in its penetrating beam. But his regard never lighted on the woman by his side. In similar fashion, Annemarie Nestor kept her eyes carefully directed away from her husband.

I wondered at the anomaly of two such striking people bound together but so coolly disengaged.

For a crowd this size, the noise level was minimal. I wasn't hoping for any outbursts or actual danger, but the evening seemed destined for boredom until a trio of late arrivals revved up the party.

I recognized Brina's pal, the bank teller Pinky Michel, as soon as she stepped from the black El Dorado. The two men in shoulder-length dreadlocks escorting her from the curb were strangers, but their identical faces gave me a clue. So I wasn't surprised when Brina introduced the Dreyfus twins as she kissed her friend.

"Pinky, you didn't tell me you were going to be here!" Brina quivered with excitement, her curls bouncing in time with the silver fish earrings.

"Yeah, well, you didn't tell me either. So I guess we're even."

Both women laughed at the lucky coincidence and hugged some more. Brina's arms only reached halfway around, her fingers squeezing the vines of sequins and beads that crawled over the red sheath dress encasing Pinky's ample frame. Her gold chandelier earrings and fiercely gelled orange spikes won Brina's top accolade: "Cute, girl! You are on fire tonight!" To me Pinky's makeup looked like war paint—thick streaks of color that obscured rather than enhanced her attractive freckles. But my views were irrelevant, so I kept my mouth shut.

I thought the silent twins looked impatient with all this unprofitable female intimacy. Scowls creased their handsome faces, and one of them reached for their employee's elbow to guide her inside.

"Come on, Pinky, we're late. You can gossip with your girlfriend after the set is over." The tenor of the voice was light, but I thought there was some menace in it too. I realized then that Pinky wasn't at the Nestor housewarming as a guest; she was the hired entertainment.

To confirm my suspicions, at that moment Sebastian Nestor bounded over to give a soul salute of bumped fists to one of the Dreyfuses and a clap on the shoulder to the other. He pecked Pinky on both cheeks, taking care not to get makeup on his face. Then he steered the trio toward the bow windows at the front of the parlor and with a flourish flung his arm in the direction of the Steinway. Dreyfus Number One took a seat at the piano, and Dreyfus Number Two plucked a microphone out of thin air and handed it to Pinky.

Sebastian's raised voice demanded attention, and the crowd hushed in an instant. Someone dimmed the living room overheads, creating a spotlight on Pinky as she stood next to her host. Her lowered head and hands clasped reverently around the mic gave an elevated theatricality to the moment.

Nestor's introduction was effusive:

"My friends, you know me as someone who's always on the lookout for the new and the next. So it is my extreme pleasure to welcome into my home a sensational young singer who is sure to capture your hearts the way she captured mine. I met her for the first time just a few short weeks ago, when I took in a show at that sizzling new hot spot, Jumeaux. You all know the Dreyfus brothers, I'm sure."

Here, Sebastian pointed at both men, bowing slightly in each direction. The crowd applauded with polite little palm smacks, and I noticed more than a few people narrow their eyes in puzzlement. Maybe the Dreyfus twins were not as well known beyond the boundaries of Harlem as their host thought. From my spot behind the crowd, I looked for Annemarie Nestor's blond head. I wanted to see if she shared her husband's enthusiasm for the Harlem music scene. Not finding her, I turned my attention back to Sebastian. Oblivious, he continued heaping on the praise, a conqueror entranced with his own arrival in an undiscovered new land.

"Their previous clubs set the standard for swank, funk, and uptown cool. Now the Dreyfus boys have opened a sizzling new hot spot, Jumeaux. And tonight, I'm proud to have in my home a lovely talent from right here in my very own neighborhood. She's a round-the-way girl with sass and class. A soulful new voice for the new age. So my friends, please welcome, straight from an exclusive engagement at Jumeaux, Harlem's own sweet bird of song, Pinky Michel!"

The applause was a little warmer this time, and Pinky flashed her gap-toothed smile. I thought she would say a few words too, but she threw a quick look at the twin on the piano and swung straight into her act.

Pinky's singing was a revelation. Her voice rolled over us like cane syrup, rich and warm in the low notes and heart-piercingly clear when she slid into the higher registers. She began the set with a medley of Sebastian Nestor's well-known songs. The composer smiled in acknowledgment of this tribute and then slipped from the spotlight. I lost him somewhere in the shadows near the staircase. To me, Nestor's tracks had never seemed like they belonged in the American songbook, too ugly and clanking with modernity. But now, Pinky smoothed out the jangling edges of his work. Her insightful arrangements exposed the wounded soul beneath Nestor's cranky lyrics and discordant notes.

Then without a pause, she switched to older favorites by Cole Porter, Hoagy Carmichael, and Nina Simone. The transition felt utterly natural, one generation of American songs speaking to another with this graceful interpreter as our guide. Bluesy or pop, jazzy or spiritual, Pinky commanded the songs and insisted on the coherence of their connection. She gave herself to us, and the crowd and the songs belonged to her.

After twenty-five minutes, Pinky's concert took yet another turn. She stopped and then bowed in the direction of the Dreyfus on the piano to thank him for his polished accompaniment. When the audience mixed calls for an encore with raucous applause, Pinky spoke a few words of introduction for this new direction. She said that the next songs were her own compositions, and she begged our forgiveness for placing her own simple works in the storied company of Porter and Nestor.

Surprising me, Pinky's songs were blues, in the tradition of Ma Rainey and Bessie Smith. Her themes were somber, but the rhythm was so rollicking and the words so raunchy that the audience chortled with joyful recognition. If anything, I thought that Pinky turned out to be a finer blues woman than a classical pop stylist. She had a gift for making you feel you had already met the people she was talking about:

I got a no-good woman,
Who went and done me wrong.
I got a no-good woman,
Who went and done me wrong.
I got a no-good woman,
And I'm good and glad
I shot her dead.

She had coal-black eyes
And lips made for a song.
Yeah, she had coal-black eyes
And lips made for a song.
She had coal-black eyes.
I'm good and glad
I put that bullet in her head.

Pinky's voice demanded vengeance, and she knew how to get it. Her lyrics made me want to kill someone; her moans made me want to cry. When the set was over, sustained applause shook the house.

As Brina wriggled forward through the crowd that crushed around Pinky, I slipped out to the kitchen looking for a glass of water. After that singing, I needed to cool off: smoky bourbon drizzled over a single cube of ice was just the thing. But I was on the job, so water had to do.

Annemarie Nestor leaned on the milky-white marble of the kitchen island, a slender hand supporting her chin. At her elbow, a small hinged evening bag lay on the counter. The purse was shaped like a fantastical bird with jewels festooned along its wings and a thin chain slinking beside it. She didn't greet me with anything warmer than a tip of the head, but when I turned in a complete circle, she remembered to be a hostess and spoke up.

"Can I help you with something?"

"Just looking for a glass of water. I think that singing just drained me of everything I've got." I hoped I sounded friendly rather than spooky.

"Water's in the tap. Glasses in the cabinet over the dishwasher. At least, I think that's where they are. They could be next to the sink. Who knows?"

When I looked puzzled, she waved her free hand over her head in an arc encompassing the whole room.

"Our cook is commander of the kitchen. She puts the dishes where she needs them, the pots where she can find them, and no one to gainsay her. Tova's a pretty fierce character, so defying her is out of the question. Com-fucking-pletely. I rarely come in here without her permission, you know. And even then..."

As her words slurred into a low mumble, I moved around the island to stand closer. Heavy lids, trembling fingers, an unruly voice whose Nordic accent had thickened with the alcohol in her blood. She was drunk, probably thrown into a melancholy funk by the last half of Pinky's concert. The blues will do that to you.

I moved a step closer. "Mrs. Nestor, do you need some help?" I trusted she was too far gone to recognize the irony of my turning her question back on her.

"You're the security man, aren't you?" She peered at me, raking her gaze over my face and then down my body.

"And do you have a name, Mr. Security Man?"

When I nodded, she closed her lids and then opened them with slow deliberation, like she was trying to hold herself erect from the inside out.

"You can call me Rook."

"And if I call you, Mr. Rook, will you come?"

Her watery smile and raised eyebrows suggested this was a skewed attempt at flirtation. She confirmed my guess by leaning closer and shifting a hand from her own chin to mine. Her fingers felt clammy, as if she had been trapped in a dank basement for a few hours. I laid her hand flat on the marble counter, as gently as I could, but it still came off like a rejection.

"You need to lie down, Mrs. Nestor. Let me go find your husband for you. He can help you get to bed."

She laughed then, a low rumble that caved in her chest and sent temblors through her throat.

"That's funny. You're funny, Mr. Security Man. You know, if you decide to give up security, you could be a comedian." None of this was said with humor, and a long sniff ended the ramble.

At that Annemarie grabbed the little jeweled purse and lifted off from the island. She slipped into a bathroom hidden behind a panel under the staircase.

I scrounged around until I found a highball glass in the cabinet above the dishwasher. As Annemarie had suggested, I ran tap water until it cooled and filled the glass. By the time I had gulped all the water, I was wondering if she would return to the kitchen to continue our flirtation or head straight upstairs. I had a clear view of the bathroom door, so I knew she hadn't emerged yet. When a man approached the bathroom and tapped on the door, I let him know that it was occupied. We waited another four minutes together, the silence growing more stilted as we dawdled.

I glanced down then and noticed that the sliver of light under the door had disappeared. I'd never heard of a woman attending to anything personal in a pitch-dark bathroom, so I knocked. Then I rattled the door handle. Nothing. I called Annemarie's name and pounded on the door. Still nothing. The inelegance of the situation evaporated as adrenaline shot through my veins. This wasn't social awkwardness; this was danger.

I jerked on the door handle three times as a crowd gathered behind me. The fourth pull broke the catch, and the door fell back. Annemarie Nestor was curled on the floor of the bathroom, her head under the tiny stainless-steel sink, her feet crammed in the space between the toilet bowl and the wall. The bejeweled purse lay gape-mouthed in a corner.

When I tugged at the collar of her sweater, it peeled up to reveal a bare swath of her chalk white torso. I dragged her across the threshold, and then sitting on the floor, I cradled her head in my lap. She was unconscious but still breathing. Her chest rose in ragged intervals, her eyes rolled back into her skull, and her mouth twisted like a ghastly scar. A bubble of saliva caught on the edge of her lower lip. A hypodermic needle jutted from the crook of her elbow. I could see a ruby drop of blood clinging to the entry wound on her ivory flesh.

"Call nine one one! You! Do it now!" Directing this order at the man nearest to me sparked him into action.

The rest of the crowd began shrieking in a useless chorus of pleas and prayers. Some pulled out cell phones, not to call for help, but to record the scene for posterity—or feed it to the ravenous Internet.

Emerging from the horde, Brina knelt beside me, her voice a balm of coherence and order.

"Rook, what happened? Is she alive?"

"She's alive; her pulse is thready, but it's there. She's overdosed on something. I don't know what she took. But I know she'd been drinking before she shot up, so the combination is dangerous."

Sebastian Nestor dropped to his knees next to me, his eyes careening wildly and his mouth open to scream. Brina cut him off by relaying the news I had just given her. She ordered again that the medics be called and the police too. Nestor's mouth clamped shut at this, but he dragged his phone from a pocket and thumbed in the number.

After that, the grim gears of tragedy and the law meshed in their familiar rotation. The police moved quickly, the medics even faster. The guests scurried away, mumbling good wishes as they fled.

The hypodermic needle was bagged and sent to the hospital lab for expedited processing.

Medics cradled Annemarie Nestor's limp body into the ambulance and sped her to the emergency room of a nearby hospital. Sebastian Nestor crouched in the back of the vehicle, bent over his stricken wife, his face a rigid mask of grief and guilt.

Hours later, Brina and I sat side by side on the steps of the Nestors' house after everyone had disappeared. The wind had picked up, swirling the leaves along the street with a scratchy noise that sounded sinister after the dire turn of events in the dark building behind us.

I held her hand, and she lay her head on my shoulder.

She was shivering. I wanted to hold her, to press her to my chest. But instead I just draped my arm around her waist. This calamity felt like my fault somehow. Like I was supposed to foresee it, prevent it, or at least intervene quicker. Annemarie hadn't reached out to me, not directly, but still the incoherent dread of her final flirtation ate away at me.

Brina caught my mood and tried to calm my lacerating thoughts.

"Rook, you can't blame yourself. There really wasn't anything you could do to prevent this, you know." Her voice echoed harshly in the empty street, but I knew she meant it to be comforting all the same. It was.

"Maybe. But that doesn't take away the horror of it."

She looked up at me with tears brimming along her reddened eyelids. Other tears had dried in faint tracks down both cheeks.

"Why, Rook? What would drive her to want to die like that?"

"I can't answer that. I doubt we'll ever know for sure."

"So what made her do this? Jealousy? Despair?" Brina shook her head. "She should have just kicked his skinny ass to the curb and left him."

I shifted my shoulders and puffed out a small sigh. My breath froze in the chilly air.

"Maybe she tried, Brina. Maybe she just couldn't do it."

Brina turned her face up to me, and we kissed again. This time the embrace was deep and complete, an antidote to the misery and hopelessness we had witnessed a few hours before.

Cupping her jaw, my fingers grazed the silver earrings. They clinked and pinged in merry counterpoint to our gloom.

"I never told you how I got these earrings, did I?" Was Brina changing the subject to divert me or propelling the conversation down the path it was already on? I couldn't be sure.

"No. Tell me."

"My mother gave them to me. Her name was Jayla Dream Ross. I called her Dreamie. Not Mommy or Mama. Just Dreamie, as though she was a sister instead of my mother. One day, I was maybe ten, Dreamie came home with a wad of purple tissue paper crumpled up in her fist. She handed the tissue paper ball to me—just tossed it in my lap really. When

I pulled out these amazing silver fish earrings, she said she had seen them on the table of a street vendor. She said she bought them because they seemed to fit me. She didn't say why she thought that. Or even if she found the earrings beautiful. Just that they reminded her of me somehow."

A hitching sob shuddered through Brina's body, and I hugged her closer.

"I mean, what was this gift supposed to be anyway? Did I remind her of a fish? Or a mermaid? Or what exactly?"

"Did you ask her?"

"Oh yeah, of course. You know how little kids are. I kept asking her, kept nagging at her. Badgering and badgering for an answer every chance I could. She never gave me one. Until one day, I guess she couldn't take the nagging anymore. So she slapped me across my cheek. Not hard, you know. It didn't really hurt, just surprised me. But hard enough to leave a red mark that lasted until Daddy came home that evening."

"What did he say?"

"You know, I never found out what he said to Dreamie. He told me to pay it no mind, to forget about it. That I was his baby, and she wouldn't do it again. Four months later Dreamie took off, and we never saw her after that."

I murmured nonsense sounds into her hair, syllables of solace for the little girl and the grown woman too. I knew more than I would admit to her about losing a parent early; my father's absence ran like a frayed thread throughout my life, unraveling or knotting up when I could least afford the weakness.

"For a long time, I thought she'd disappeared because of me. That somehow, I'd cast a spell that caused Dreamie to just vanish. Poof. You know, magical thinking the way kids do. My father looked for her, but nothing came of it. Finally, he just quit searching."

Lots of people go missing in Harlem, Brina had told me. We find the ones who want to be found. The rest, well, they stay lost. I wondered if she really believed it. Or was this just a saying she wielded like a talisman to ward off grief and explain away failure.

"But you still wear the earrings, Brina. Why is that?" I stroked my thumbs over the tear tracks on her cheeks.

"I don't know exactly. I guess because they remind me of Dreamie. Of times when she was kind and that she loved me once."

With that sorrow pressing down, I couldn't think of words for what I wished she would believe about me, about the us we might become together. So I stuck with phrases I'd used earlier in the evening. I told her the silver fish earrings were beautiful, and she was beautiful too. I hoped that was enough.

Chapter 4
THE CRYSTAL-CLEAR BLESSING

"Junior, I'll only give you this piece of country advice once. Brina's a grown woman, but she's still a little girl. So don't push too hard, or she'll run like the dickens. But you hang back like some kind of nervous clown, and she'll run even faster. So go for it, but don't be a fool, you understand?"

Chapter 5
THE BIG YELLOW CAT

A week after the Nestor housewarming party, we learned that doctors had discovered that Annemarie's overdose was due to a massive injection of insulin. I understood the insulin caused a severe insult to the brain. They guessed that the injection I'd witnessed at the party was the last of several Annemarie had taken that day. Mixed with a significant amount of alcohol, the insulin poisoning was grave, but the emergency-room staff saved her life. Her brain function was impaired, but exactly how much I never found out.

The insulin belonged to her husband, who was diabetic. Knowing this, I thought Annemarie's gesture seemed all the more desperate and defiant, like she'd rolled up a lifetime of contempt and accusation in a ball and hurled it at him.

"Look, you did what you could for her." Brina stopped pacing the length of my office and turned in front of the window to stare at me.

I knew she wanted to snatch me out of my brooding. She was growing impatient with my inability to shake off the last case.

"Annemarie Nestor would be dead if you hadn't dragged her out of that bathroom just when you did. Their mess isn't on you, Rook. It's on that creep Sebastian. So let it go."

Brina halted in front of me and slapped a file folder on my desk. The sharp whack suggested the noise a flat palm might make against an unguarded cheek, so I sat forward in my chair and raised my eyebrows to show I was paying attention.

"Tomorrow night we're on duty at a town-hall meeting at the high-school auditorium. Read about it here. Or duck out if you want to keep on wallowing. Your choice."

I speared the folder with an index finger and dragged it to me. "I'm in."

The assignment seemed a simple one. The Ross Agency had been hired to provide quiet backup for the uniformed police contingent guarding a community gathering.

Local politicians, including state-assembly representatives, school board leaders, and city-council members, had organized a meeting to address constituent concerns on a hot new issue: gentrification. Of course, no one had dropped perennial worries about gang violence, illegal drugs, police mistreatment, or shoddy school buildings. The community suffered from a multitude of plagues that hadn't disappeared since the last election. But changing demographics were sparking a new kind of fear, an existential pressure roiling the collective mind of the neighborhood: If Harlem turned white, could it still claim to be the capital of Black America?

Gentrification was the catchphrase for this boiling worry. Block by block, elders sold their homes to white pioneers with fat purses. Liquor stores and bodegas vanished overnight, replaced by wine boutiques and frozen-yogurt shops. Ugly diners cinderella'd into cupcake emporiums, which morphed into elegant cafés whose prices curled the processed hair of longtime residents.

Answers weren't going to descend from heaven or city hall at this meeting, of course. No one expected simple resolutions to be the end product of a single session. But community leaders hoped that by bringing together all corners of Harlem, everyone would have a chance to air his or her concerns—landlords and developers, homeowners and renters, retailers and restaurateurs, longtime residents and newly arrived neighbors, everybody talking it out in frank exchanges, if not in downright harmony.

The town-hall meeting was certain to be contentious. The organizers hoped the Ross Agency could keep the conversation safe, civil, and orderly. I thought it might be a tough assignment, so I was glad we were only going to provide support for the regular forces. But Brina told me the organizers wanted to minimize the visible presence of the police, fearing they might incite disturbances rather than quell them.

According to Brina, we were supposed to be discreet, unobtrusive, and nonconfrontational. When we arrived at the high-school auditorium the following evening, I thought she and I did a good job of blending in with the crowd. A black pullover for me and a long multicolored wool cardigan for her made our no-name jeans look modest and unhip.

But Norment Ross wore a suit of maroon velvet that mimicked the upholstery on the two hundred seats in the theatre. The summer straw fedora had been replaced by a houndstooth-checkered driving cap, its cloth playing a pun on his midnight skin and snow-white goatee. Ross looked like a red-cloaked panther, alert and sleek. He prowled the aisle on the right side of the auditorium while I hung back next to the doors at the rear of the center aisle. Brina stationed herself on the left corridor, about halfway toward the raised stage at the front of the theatre.

Soon every seat in the auditorium was filled; the place steamed and bubbled with our communal energy. Given the evening's subject matter, I thought the crowd seemed boisterous but still cordial. People shouted greetings down the rows, saluted acquaintances, or stood to pose for selfies. Babies bounced on knees or were passed around for kisses. Gladhanding and flirting seemed the preferred activities, although I could see many people with notebooks and pens so I knew the socializing would soon give way to business.

I recognized several people in the gathering: Pinky Michel had brought one of the enterprising Dreyfus twins as an escort; I wasn't sure which one. Mrs. Abernathy, minus her yellow cat Peaches, took a seat in the first row. On the left-hand aisle near Brina's position, I sighted my favorite waitress, Raye, and her partner Lonnie. Raye, festive in a canary-yellow bob, twisted around in her seat to wave at me and rolled her eyes toward

Brina, signaling some message I couldn't readily translate. I glimpsed four of the dignitaries from Ross's whist playing club. With two winks, a tap on the eyebrow, and a genuine grin, the old boys acknowledged my presence. Seeing so many people I knew made me feel I was part of this community too, that I had a stake in its future, even after only a few short months here.

The arrangement of the space was designed to encourage talk: three microphones were mounted on tall stands at the head of each aisle. A long table on the stage was cluttered with dignitaries jostling for the limelight. But in opening remarks, the master of ceremonies promised that after each politician had spoken for one minute, audience members would have a chance to ask questions from the floor. Of course, the officials couldn't pass up the opportunity to preach to a crowd of voters, so their allotments of one minute each soon stretched to two, and in a few cases, the MC had to cut off the speeches to prevent the restive crowd from storming the stage.

Finally, it was the people's turn to speak. I studied the sweaty faces in the long lines that snaked away from each microphone. I didn't know precisely what I was expecting. What did an agitator look like anyway? What constituted actual danger in this tense atmosphere? Must exhaustion inevitably cross over into fury? Did indignation have to convert into rage? I was on the lookout for something, but what it was eluded me. The parade of speakers moved on in a seemingly endless display. Some confined themselves to short statements or passionate questions. A few whined and a few wept. Others descended into screeching diatribes that elicited catcalls or thunderous stamping of feet.

I perked up at one point when a scrawny young man flaunting a big Afro asked about the fire at the Auberge Rouge. With a sneer curling his mouth, he demanded to know if the politicians and police believed that arson was an acceptable method of gentrifying Harlem. The crowd booed and hissed at the limp responses from the stage. I had no intention of speaking up about my personal experiences; I didn't figure anybody here really cared to hear my story. But the mention of the Rouge did strengthen my sense that, however tenuous it might be, I had indeed earned a place in this community.

The clotted heat and the repetitive harangues fogged my mind as the hours crawled by. I was just about to step through the doors into the lobby to clear the haze from my head when an arresting young woman approached the microphone in the center aisle. Though she appeared to be no more than thirty years old, she wore a vintage dress in burgundy satin with a nipped-in waist over a skirt that flared out dramatically to her knees. She had sculpted her frizzy hair into an elaborate halo of folds around her head. When I stopped my retreat to listen to her speech, I noticed a small boy hiding his face in the pleats of her dress.

"Many of you on the stage this evening have told us what you intend to do to our neighborhood. You have used the term 'rehabilitation' to describe your plans. But we are *not* sick. We are *not* injured. We are *not* wounded. We don't need rehabilitation because we are *not* a community of deficit."

Here the crowd rose, applauding, and she paused to let them settle before continuing. Sincerity glowed from her bare face, her dark eyes radiating a rare honesty that touched every willing soul in the theatre.

"We have imagination and drive and courage and heart. Feed our spirit, and we will make Harlem sing. We don't need Sencha tea; we have pot liquor! We don't want basil-lime ice cream; we have sweet-potato pie in abundance! Feed our soul, and we will make Harlem thrive!"

Shouts of "Yes!" and "Preach, sister!" punctuated these comments as the crowd pounded the armrests and stamped the floor. The roar of approval resolved into a chant as the young woman turned from the microphone: "Thrive, thrive, thrive." The crowd was ready to follow her up any hill she chose—she only had to ask. But the young woman just hoisted her son to her hip and pushed on until she reached her seat again. The sight of her serene brown face seemed to flood the room with certainty. Rather than arousing her neighbors to violence, her simple words seemed to have spread a balm over the troubled crowd, instilling a new sense of hope. Tension ebbed from the space, and I looked toward Brina to see if she too sensed the changed mood. It felt as though our work was done.

As the throng parted to let their new champion pass, I caught sight of a familiar head moving on my left toward the rear of the auditorium. The string cheese comb-over still straggled across the pale scalp. Watery gray eyes rolled in their usual pattern as the face oscillated from side to side. Larry Sherman, unsavory landlord and Harlem fixture, slithered out of the room.

I wasn't going to let him escape. I felt a twinge of anxiety as I left Brina and Ross behind in the auditorium. We were a team, and I was skipping out on an assignment. I felt sure any danger had passed, but I knew I'd catch hell, particularly from Brina, for this breach of trust. I was putting myself on shaky ground with her at a point where I couldn't afford to lose her confidence or commitment.

But tracking Larry Sherman took precedence now. I would explain my disappearance later.

———

I trailed Sherman for six blocks. At first, I feared he would jump into a car, and I would have to settle for a license plate number instead of an address for my quarry. But he kept on walking, and so did I. Bone-chilling gusts propelled him along the avenues, fists stuffed in his jacket pockets; if I was cold in my wool sweater, he must be frigid in his flimsy windbreaker. A change in the weather, which had been unsettled for several weeks, gripped the city at last. The late October wind had stiffened after sunset, scattering flame-colored leaves that had collected along the cracked sidewalks. My foot ached with the unyielding cement and the fast march Sherman set. After a half hour of trudging, Sherman suddenly kicked aside a pile of leaves and crept up the steps of a familiar gray-stone apartment building. I had been here before but never seen Larry Sherman on the premises.

As he rattled a key in the door, I leaned behind a tree at the curb. I noticed a bright window to the right of the entrance. The first-floor occupants had not yet lowered their living-room window against the night air. Lounging in perfect comfort just inside the sill was a big yellow cat, his paws curled under his chest, a satisfied smile curving his whiskers and triangular ears alert. I recognized this haughty sentinel even before he opened his yellow lantern eyes: I had picked up Peaches from the back porch of this apartment only a few weeks ago. This was the cheating cat's second home.

Peaches recognized me too. When I ran up to stop the front door from slamming shut behind Sherman, the cat sprang into a bristling arch and spat a warning. Hisses and an angry shriek followed the spitting. Peaches, now armored with spikes of fur and blazing eyes, was in full battle mode. Sherman's head jerked around at the commotion. That hesitation gave me enough time to push my shoulder into the gap and force Larry back into the narrow lobby.

Sherman shrank against the bank of metal mailboxes on one wall of the vestibule. His tone was every bit as hostile as Peaches's had been:

"What are you doing here? You following me?"

"Yeah, I followed you, Larry. Tracked you down. You didn't exactly leave a forwarding address the last time we saw each other."

"Leave me alone. You got no right, no *right* to harass me like this." Sherman shriveled into a corner, but I followed him right into it, until our chests met and my chin touched the front of his pasty brow.

"That's funny. Real funny, Larry. The way I figure it, you owe me six hundred dollars for a security deposit."

"You don't get no back rent, Rook. Seeing how it was the fire, not me, that booted you out of the Rouge. Act of God. I don't have no control over that, and you know it."

I didn't mention the police and the insurance company investigating him on possible arson charges. If Larry the Worm wanted to stick with an act-of-God defense, I wasn't going to argue the point. I just clutched the collar of his jacket and drew him closer.

"Look, I get six hundred dollars might not mean much to a big-time landlord like you. But it means a lot to me. The difference between crawling around in the dirt and getting back on my feet. So I need that money."

I paused to take a quick look around the lobby. The floor was swept clean but tiles were missing from the black-and-white pattern, and the rubber welcome mat was curled at both ends. A faceted plastic ball acted as a chandelier, casting dingy light over the room. Fingerprints soiled the mint-colored walls beside the mailboxes. The space smelled faintly of collard greens and Pine-Sol.

"And now that I know where you live, I'll be back around on a regular basis until you pay up what you owe me. You think the nice respectable tenants you have here would be happy to learn about your walk on the wild side? I could tell them about the Auberge Rouge. I could tell them all about that, if you want."

Somehow seeing Larry squirm in my grasp only increased my indignation, and I pulled his face right up to mine. That close, he smelled like mothballs and peanut butter, sweat and fear. I could feel rage pounding up toward my head: the humiliation of sleeping in an office because I couldn't afford an apartment; washing my underwear in a shared sink; owing money to Lee's for dry cleaning and to Mei Young and Lonnie's Diner for my meals. All of this churned until, in that moment, I wanted to squash the life from him. But I didn't do it. As Peaches is my witness, I wanted to, but I couldn't do it.

Larry's wheedling voice interrupted my seething, and his pathos calmed me somehow. "Look, you don't need to do that, do you?" My threat had hit gut, as much gut as the Worm possessed.

"OK, Larry. You know, I'm a reasonable man. I can give you time. In fact, why don't we work it like this: you can pay me back when you collect on the fire insurance policy."

I was fishing, but Larry seemed primed to spike himself on the hook.

"OK. That's a deal. I can settle up with you at the end of next month when my insurance check comes in."

Larry paused, his eyes scurrying back and forth. Then he ran a putty-colored hand through his hair, making the strands stick up from his scalp.

"Say, how'd you know I'd be getting an insurance payout anyway?" Confusion bubbled across his face.

"I didn't. Until you just told me, Larry."

At that, red seeped into the sickly gray on his sunken cheeks.

"Well, don't go spreading it around, hear? No need to give people the wrong idea like I made a profit off the Rouge or something. Believe me, there's no way to make ends meet running an operation like that. No way."

This was confirmation enough for me. Larry had as much as confessed to torching the brothel to collect insurance money. He didn't care about the lives lost or the suffering endured. He needed money, and the fire was the way to get it.

I didn't need to hear any more. I clocked Sherman good, a single stiff blow that opened a cut over his left eyebrow and sent him staggering to the tiles.

"That's for the girls of the Rouge."

Sherman spewed a few curses but stayed on the floor as I hurried down the steps to the sidewalk. I looked to see if Peaches was still on sentry duty. Although his family had closed the window against the chilly air and strange noises, the yellow cat remained on guard. He stared at me with unblinking gold-disk eyes until I crossed the street and reached the corner of the block.

———

The office was empty when I got back. In the bathroom, I ran cold water over my reddened knuckles until the stinging subsided.

A quick call to the precinct completed my assignment for the night. When I asked for them, the desk sergeant said neither Detective Lin nor Officer Nelson was around.

"You give them this address, and tell them that the Worm has turned up. They'll know what it means. No, no name. Just a concerned citizen doing his duty. You just tell 'em."

I repeated Sherman's address slowly, until I was sure the sergeant had recorded it correctly.

———

The next morning, Brina was chafed. Her eyes, usually so soft and warm, shot darts at me as we talked. Or actually, as she talked and I listened.

"You skipped out on us last night, Rook. Despite what you say, that's no small thing. You took off to pursue your own private case. You didn't check in with me or my father. You just took off. Disappeared. We have to be able to trust you, Rook. Someday our lives could depend on that trust. If you don't get that, then maybe you need to think about another job."

I didn't have much to say in reply. Her comments stung. Cut and run was not me—not me at my best anyway. I wanted to be that man Brina thought I was. The partner she hoped to find in me.

———

I expected Archibald Lin to contact me that morning, but his call didn't come until noon two days later. In terse phrases, he ordered me to join him at Larry Sherman's apartment. When I got there, squad cars were stationed at each end of the block. Uniformed cops and crime-scene technicians hustled in and out of the building, their faces grim masks of professional determination. Lin met me on the front step, and once past the lobby, he lifted the yellow tape that barricaded the doorway of the basement apartment so that we could descend together.

Larry Sherman was sprawled in a recliner chair in the sitting room of the apartment. The raised footrest and angled chair back suggested Larry was relaxing to catch a game on TV. An open beer can nestled in a convenient slot in the armrest. A half-empty bag of Fritos chips lay crumpled on the floor next to the chair. But Larry's mouse-colored eyes stared into nothing. And a hole crusted with dried blood gaped in the middle of his chest.

"You think he looks surprised? Like the guy came at him all of a sudden?"

These were the first sentences Lin spoke to me. I couldn't tell if his tone was accusatory or not. I knew that the two inches of raw split skin above Larry's brow belonged to me, but I didn't want to confess that to the police right away. Or ever.

I looked again at Larry's face. The skin's normal gray had molted into a downy beige, mottled and sagging without the guile that had animated it before. His mouth drooped at both corners where spittle had dried into a white lace. I had despised Larry Sherman in life, but I hated his death even more.

"Jeez, I don't know, Lin. He didn't look like this when I left him, I can tell you that. When I left, Larry was breathing. And cursing. And promising to pay me my money when the insurance came in. He was breathing. That's all I can tell you."

Lin pointed to a corner of the room where a small wooden table lay belly-up, a drawer pulled-out half way. Keys, coupons, rubber bands, a roll of stamps, and a cell-phone charger were scattered around.

"Looks like Sherman was stabbed over there near the kitchen entrance. He was facing his assailant, so it looks like Larry let him in the front door, maybe talked for a bit, then walked toward the kitchen, and then turned around all of a sudden. Took three blows to the chest. Smaller than a butcher knife but bigger than a switch blade. Fell on the carpet here."

During this description, Lin acted out the part of the hapless Larry, moving through the room with a delicate agility that belied his bulk.

I could see where this sketch was going, so I finished off the gruesome scenario. "Then the guy dragged Larry over to the chair and posed him like this? What for?"

"I don't know. Thought you'd have a theory. In view of you being the last person to see Sherman alive."

"Except for his killer."

We let that hang in the air for another minute. I didn't like being accused of murder, even in this indirect way. But I could see how I might fit into Lin's developing theory of the crime. I had opportunity, and being enraged about the back rent might be motive enough. Tough luck my only corroborating witness was a big yellow cat who hated my guts.

"Look, if I killed Larry, why would I go to the trouble of setting up the room like this? Then phone in the address to give you guys a heads-up? You may not like me, but you can't believe I'm that crazy or that stupid."

I paused to see if Lin was buying what I was selling. He nodded, so I continued.

"And if I killed him, what did I use for a weapon? Are any of the knives missing from the kitchen? No? Then did I come here already carrying a weapon? Meaning I had to have planned the murder before I even discovered where Larry lived. Or did I come back later to kill him, taking the risk that you or Nelson would already be following up on my tip? That makes no sense, and you know it."

As I unwound the absurd hypothesis, my vocal chords tightened until my voice sounded like a screech crossed with a cackle.

Lin's face took on a familiar sly expression, like he'd won a game I didn't realize we were playing. "Yeah, that's where I come out too, Rook. I just wanted to see you squirm a little."

With the smug bastard staring me down, I couldn't very well wipe the sweat from my upper lip right then, although I wanted to. To distract him, I threw out a question before I flicked a finger across my mouth.

"So how long do you figure Sherman's been dead?"

"The medical examiner gets the last word, but my guess is we're looking at about twelve hours, maybe less."

"Around one a.m. this morning, you figure."

"Yeah, more or less." After a minute of silence, Lin's expression grew mournful. I thought he might be gearing up to offer a brief eulogy for the late Larry Sherman. I was wrong.

"You know, the Worm getting killed like this blows a big hole in our idea that he was responsible for the fire at the Auberge Rouge."

"Kind of thoughtless of him to go and get himself murdered like that, huh, Lin?"

"Yeah, real inconvenient. After that town-hall meeting two nights ago, the community agitators are up in arms. They want answers on the

Auberge Rouge. The lieutenant's going to chew my ass off and spit it out in little bits."

"I'd pay to see that."

Lin let me go soon after. As I walked back to the agency, I wondered if anyone out there was looking for Larry Sherman, if even one person cared that he'd gone missing. Larry hadn't done much for me when he lived, but he'd been the first person I'd met when I arrived in Harlem. He deserved a far better death than the one he got.

Chapter 6
THE SCARLET DOOR

I've never been in the tropics. Except for that one time a botched road trip to Disney World dumped me on a spit of land off Key West, minus my wife.

But looking down from my spy perch, the women fluttering out of the cavernous maw of an old Harlem church looked like tropical birds to me. Stationed at the window on the second-floor landing of a gray stone apartment building opposite the church, I had a panoramic view of the parade below.

Down the steps they skittered in fantastical garments of turquoise, honey, scarlet, lime, and lilac. Their outfits were topped by matching hats encrusted with lace and feathers and beads drooping over brims that swept from shoulder to shoulder. The display was delicious; it was old fashioned in its color-coordinated intricacy, and the thin November Sunday light enhanced the air of lush exuberance.

These women looked powerful, inaccessible, and gorgeous in their gleaming black skins. I recognized cat-lady Mrs. Carla Abernathy in the crowd, but the others were imposing strangers.

The theatrical excess of the scene awed me, and I was glad to be only an observer of the dazzling scene. A skinny café-con-leche tinted man in black slacks and black pullover sweater wasn't going to cut it on Harlem's walk of glory this brisk morning. But I was sure Brina, graceful, effortless Brina, would fit into this impressive congregation without much more than a shake of her elegant shoulders if—big if—she ever bothered to get her Afro-bohemian self out of bed in time to make it to church.

The ladies' distant chattering wafted up from the street, sounds bright and perky enough to keep me awake, but lacking enough definition or coherence to reignite the headache I had shed just an hour ago. I'd been here for over ninety minutes, waiting for a quiet moment to enter the apartment of my latest target, because I'd decided that a visit before noon on Sunday would not be welcomed or even possible given the throbbing state of my bourbon-drenched brain.

When Old Man Ross dispatched me on this assignment, he hadn't handed over much more than a few crumbs in the way of background. I knew the initial inquiry came from the landlady of this building. According to Ross, she was nosy about all her tenants, naturally. But the day she came to the agency, she had blood on her mind. Frothing with suspicion, she claimed to have heard weird snatches of conversation coming from the upper apartment of her property. I hadn't met the landlady in person—Ross or Brina handled all the client contacts for our tiny operation. I supplied the eyes, ears, or muscle as needed. But Ross conveyed the gist of the new case in his usual telegraphic style: Mrs. Busybody was convinced that one of her apartment's tenants planned to murder the other.

According to Ross's sketchy information, my current target was an elderly man who lived on one of the premiere streets in the Strivers' Row neighborhood of Harlem near St. Nicholas Park, just a few doors away from the Nestors' ill-fated house. Ross felt confident that because of his advanced age, the man could not be considered a threat to anyone else, so he must be the victim of the violent plot the landlady was sure she had overheard.

Norment Ross had good instincts and a moral compass that always pointed true. After forty years of plying the detective trade in Harlem, he could read a person or a situation with unmatched ease. Brina was almost as skilled as her father in this regard. With a gimlet eye for the disguised tell, she could divine who was pulling a con and who was just pulling a leg and who was in danger and who was in denial. Though Boss Ross was the natural skeptic in the family, it was Brina who usually delivered the no that kept their business solvent and their heads securely connected to their necks.

Months after joining the agency, I still puzzled over my good luck. Against every expectation, I was still around, working cases, wondering how I managed to stick.

The only blueprints of the building's interior that Brina could locate dated to its construction in 1895, so I wasn't sure of the current layout of the apartment. I could tell as soon as I hit the front door that the original arrangement of the residence as a single-family townhouse had been divided some time ago. I knew that my target lived in the upper two floors of the four-story building.

I knocked on the richly lacquered scarlet door five times. A flicker of light shone through the peep hole, and I knew I was being examined. So I schooled my face into an innocent expression I hoped was winning enough to gain entrance.

After a few uncomfortable moments, the door swung open, and the observer swept a long arm in an arc of welcome.

I entered and turned immediately to launch into the cover story I had decided upon as an explanation for my visit. Even to my own ears, the notion that I was the representative of an insurance company seeking to verify the claimants to a lapsed policy sounded fake.

I wouldn't believe the feeble story, and I doubted the old gentleman standing before me did either.

But my host was gracious and led me without question toward the front of the apartment to a space designed as a reception room or parlor.

I know nothing about architecture, but I could recognize the calm elegance of the room's proportions and appreciate the delicate moldings framing the cream-colored ceiling. The wood paneling that rose as high as my shoulders ran along all four walls. I was impressed with the oak fireplace, which was decorated with small green and white glazed tiles.

A shiny grand piano dominated one corner of the room. Next to it were four stacks of white folding chairs, poised as if in anticipation of a great audience.

The windows overlooking the street formed a bay that was completed by high-backed window benches in black wood. This was where the old man led me and indicated I should sit down.

"Now that you have that cock-and-bull story out of your system, young man, I hope we can have a civil conversation."

The tone was cordial and crisp, in a lilting tenor voice that took decades off the appearance of its owner.

I found myself at ease and amused by my canny host. I felt I should keep up some sort of barrier between us, if only to protect myself and my assignment. But the effort was tough, and the more I examined him, the more I wanted to drop the pretense.

The man was at least six feet four, narrow and straight as a plum line, with the smoothest skin and whitest hair I had ever seen. The hair rose in a great cottony crown above the long bronze face that was punctuated by a white mustache clipped with military precision.

He carried a slender staff of polished wood, an inch taller than he was. But he didn't seem to lean on it for support, so I guessed that the walking stick was a theatrical embellishment more than a crutch.

The closest I could come to describing the man's outfit was as a caftan, in a lightweight fabric with a garish pattern of gold, orange, black, and green. The deep green was picked up again in the embroidery that garnished the neckline and sleeve openings of the garment.

I wanted to commit all these details to memory so that I could share them with Brina later.

"I'm sorry..." was all that I managed before the man launched into a tirade that warmed my heart even as it pretended to chastise me for my false bona fides.

"I suppose you are either peddling subscriptions to the Watchtower or selling cookies to raise funds for a charitable cause. I must warn you that I have been converted at least twelve times over my life span, and none of them ever took.

"Perhaps you will have better luck today than your fellow religion pushers."

I tried to interject.

"No, I'm not…"

"And I must further warn you that I am a master baker. I have the blue ribbons from county fairs all over eastern Pennsylvania to prove it. So, I have no need for your packaged Scout cookies full of dubious chemicals and strange admixtures.

"In any event, I wouldn't buy a cookie or a new religion from a complete stranger, mister…?"

"You can call me Ryder." For some reason, giving him the name Rook right off the bat felt wrong.

"Well, Mr. Ryder. My name is Andrew Arthur Austin. My parents had a sense of humor, so they called my sisters Annette, Amelia, and Adele. Their middle names also began with *A*, but I won't bore you with listing those."

The old man looked away toward the lofty ceiling as if studying the faces of his departed family and then brought his sharp brown eyes back to me.

When Austin didn't say anything further, I decided it was my turn at civil conversation.

"If you suspected I wasn't on the up and up, why did you let me in the door?"

"Oh, curiosity, I suppose. We rarely get a visitor under the age of eighty in this building. And certainly none with a face as beautiful as yours, Mr. Ryder. You have the eyes of an angel fallen to Earth, as I am sure you have been told before."

I shifted on the bench at this frank compliment.

I had a mirror, but it didn't tell me much except when to shave and how to stick a Band-Aid over a razor nick. Brina claimed I looked like the child of an impossible marriage between Ava Gardner and some pop star named Zayn Malik. I could see how Ava might account for the black hair and chin dimple, but I didn't know where the Zayn Malik influence fit in. Some people called my dark-gray eyes cold or stormy or creepy. No one, not even my mother, had ever said I had angel eyes.

"But I suppose that, sadly, you are as straight as my walking stick. What a waste!"

The old man shrugged philosophically and then laughed, maybe questioning this latest sign of the universe's mysterious ways.

"You know, Mr. Ryder. I am quite old. My birthday next month will make me one hundred and eight years old. I have seen many things you cannot begin to imagine and many more things perhaps you *can* imagine because you have seen them in the newspapers and on television. I was the first Black student—we were Negroes then—to graduate from the high school in our little town in eastern Pennsylvania. I think the only reason they tolerated me was that I was an excellent athlete and our team made it to the state finals in track for the first time ever the year I won the one-hundred-meter sprint and anchored the four-by-four relay. I also had a pretty good tenor voice, and they let me sing solos in the school choir every once in a while."

Austin didn't seem to need the stimulus of an interlocutor. My willing presence was encouragement enough, I guess.

"When I went to college it was on a music scholarship, but I didn't spend much time studying music. Too busy giving hell to the college administration for their backward policies. They tried to kick me out a few times, but since I was editor of the student newspaper, my colleagues threatened to raise an even bigger ruckus, and I managed to hang on by the skin of my teeth."

Austin paused his narrative and raised his long narrow chin high.

"I was a communist before the Spanish Civil War, Mr. Ryder, before it was fashionable among the literary set. And I was an agitator for Negro civil rights before the Pullman porters even had a union. And I was a homosexual when there was not a shred of gaiety involved. Oh, I wasn't afraid to pursue my personal desires. Not at all. But it did cost me some dear friendships."

The old man shook his woolly head and closed his eyes. I missed the fierce glow they cast and hoped my host wasn't growing too tired to continue his story.

After a moment Austin rallied.

"If you will accompany me to the kitchen, Mr. Ryder, I will make good on my earlier boast and provide you with something from the oven. I believe I have a slice or two of poppy-seed cake left over from last night, which, if I do say so myself, is delicious with my special lemon sauce."

We made our way slowly toward the rear of the apartment, the steady thump of the walking stick punctuating our passage.

The long hallway leading to the kitchen was lined with framed photographs of Austin in formal poses across many decades of changing fashion in personal attire and politics. Alternating with the portraits were mounted dust jackets of books Austin had written on subjects ranging from peace to poverty to poetry.

When we stepped on the hard tile of the kitchen, the sound seemed to send a signal to the other occupants of the apartment. Two enormous cats bounded in from somewhere beyond the kitchen, eager to persuade their master that it was lunchtime again.

"Ah, the lord and lady of the manor deign to make an appearance."

Austin bent to caress each furry triangular head and introduced them in turn.

"This is Brick. He favors me." The yellow creature with outsized paws and golden eyes looked up at Austin with apparent adoration. Then he turned a baleful glance at me and hissed. I recognized Peaches, Mrs. Abernathy's wandering cat from several previous encounters. By my count, this was the unfaithful cat's fourth home.

"And this is Maggie. She, on the other hand, is voraciously heterosexual." As if to prove it, the sleek black-and-white cat curved around my ankles and between my legs, purring furiously.

Austin cut two thick slices of cake, poured milk for humans and felines, and led me to the adjacent room, which served as both a library and a dining spot.

We sat for an hour amid the book-lined shelves and the overstuffed sofas, once red, now faded to comfortable pink. With only a little prompting from me, Austin produced a set of leather-bound scrapbooks that contained a seventy-five-year collection of photos and newspaper clippings. He laid them out on the long table and proceeded to lead me through the collection in chronological order.

I flipped through the pages feeling increasingly inadequate and lost. There were hundreds of yellowed pictures of Austin standing with men I assumed were famous but whose names meant nothing to me.

I only recognized Dr. King, Paul Robeson, and several presidents and a few athletes; the rest of the faces were apparently noteworthy figures who had made news or culture or both during the previous century but whose exploits I did not know of in any detail.

I thought of Brina again and wished she were here to look through these artifacts with me. She would know and appreciate what this history meant, I was sure. I pictured her wild cloud of curls, her graceful brown neck bent over the albums and her long fingers racing over the images and words in these dusty volumes.

Fortunately, Austin did not require anything more from me than murmured words of approval and chuffs of amusement at jokes as dusty and old as the wine-colored notebooks themselves.

Drawing my thumb along the crackled newsprint of a lengthy article in the fourth scrapbook, I was startled out of my silence.

"This is an obituary. *For you.* How is that possible?"

Austin barked a laugh, his head thrown back, his eyes closed in merriment.

"Oh, young man, I have been dead for quite a while, since 1997 to be precise!"

"What do you mean by that?"

"Well, as you can plainly read, I passed away in my sleep from a heart attack at the age of eighty-three after a long and distinguished career of service to the nation. At my request, my body was cremated, and there was no public funeral in my honor. The site of my interment was kept secret to protect my family from unwanted invasions of privacy. It's all spelled out right there."

He thumped a long index finger on the clipping to emphasize his point.

I felt unnerved by this facile explanation and impatient with the broad grin on his face.

"That makes no sense, and you know it. What really happened?"

The old man's face softened into a more somber pose.

"If you must know, Mr. Ryder. I chose some time ago to disappear from this life. It seemed the easiest way to do it was to go all at once and with finality. I had made some money from my books and speaking engagements but nothing really substantial. Some careful calculations and discreet inquiries revealed that my life-insurance policy would pay out a sizeable amount to my heir in the event of my death. That amount was enough on which to live modestly and in comfortable obscurity.

"And that is what we have done these past twenty years, Robbie and I."

"Robbie?"

"Yes, Robbie. Robert Unger. I thought you had done your homework before you came calling, Mr. Ryder."

The gentle chiding tone had returned in force, but I chose to ignore it.

"I don't know who Robert Unger is."

"I suppose you could call him my 'boyfriend,' if that term may be applied to a man just past eighty. 'Longtime companion'? So very pretentious. 'Lover' seems so athletic, and 'husband' seems excessively formal, don't you think?"

When I didn't reply, Austin continued lightly.

"Since it's only the two of us here—and the cats, of course—I just call him Robbie and let it go at that."

I was full of questions, which Austin patiently answered over the course of the next half hour.

He and Robbie had met while working in a small international peace organization that promoted community reconciliation initiatives in the Third World. Robbie was an excellent writer and a sensitive editor, skills Austin took full advantage of to improve his last three books. They fell in love; Robbie moved into the magnificent old apartment on Strivers' Row and became his legal heir.

After his "death," Austin remained in absolute seclusion. Robbie did all the shopping, the banking, and the correspondence for the couple.

Austin passed his days reading newspapers, baking, and practicing the piano. He disciplined himself to write at least one thousand words every day and had completed four book-length manuscripts, a novel, and a memoir.

"Robbie has strict instructions to burn them all when I go. But I am counting on him to be disobedient."

Austin had never left their glorious apartment in twenty-five years.

"Well, not quite never," he amended his declaration.

"I did decide to go out on the night that brilliant young man was elected president. I wanted to go down to Union Square and see the masses gathered in celebration there. Robbie was firmly against it. He said we would be trampled by the crowd. But I said, if I had to die—again—then I couldn't think of a better way to go. So we went down and had a simply marvelous time. All those young people, every color and ethnicity, tears running down all those splendid faces, the energy and joy there. It was extraordinary.

"Best night of my life, Mr. Ryder. The best night of my life."

Austin's eyes shimmered with thoughts of that historic occasion. Was he wondering again at the ways of the mysterious universe in which he alone had lived long enough to see that desired day, when all of his dear friends, the valiant ones who had worked the hardest to achieve it, had gone before him?

I let the conversation pause a moment, but I needed to press on.

"And Robbie, where is he now?"

"Oh, out hunting and gathering. I suppose. He should be back before evening. He does most of the weekly shopping on Sunday afternoon. Some weekends he takes time out to see a movie or have a drink or two at a watering hole downtown. Taking care of me is quite a burdensome occupation, as you might imagine. So I don't begrudge him his little escapades now and then."

Austin turned a shrewd eye on me.

"My dear boy, you came here with a purpose. Now is the time to divulge it. I am quite sure you won't shock me, whatever it is."

I was hesitant to speak bluntly, but I couldn't think of a way to sugar-coat my message.

"I have information that you are in danger, Mr. Austin. This information suggests that you may be killed or injured sometime in the near future."

I felt sheepish for not having more details to support my wild claim. It sounded so reasonable when Brina and Ross first told me, but now the words seemed absurd. But then I didn't really know any more than I had just offered. Ross's information was sparse, and the ultimate source of the information was dubious at best.

To my surprise, this assertion set Austin off on another round of hearty laughter. The old man clapped his graceful hands together and leaned back in his chair so far that I feared he would tumble over.

"That is marvelous, Mr. Ryder, just marvelous!"

I scowled in a way I hoped would sober up the conversation.

"I don't see what's so funny."

"Of course you don't, dear boy. The fact is, I do know that I may be killed in the near future.

"In truth, I am counting on it!"

———

Austin's laughter filled the room. Brick and Maggie were startled out of their naps by the outburst, but they quickly entangled again and sank back into sleep.

"Go on." I knew I sounded sour, but I couldn't help it. The old man's unexpected response wounded my pride somehow. Austin continued with hearty cheer.

"I had decided about six months ago that the present arrangements were really intolerable for any number of reasons. I am not in the best of health—"

"You look fine to me." The interruption was rude, but I couldn't help it.

"Yes, well thank you. But my doctor assures me I have at least twelve more months of excruciating agony ahead of me before I die. Dr. Krishna Patel, last man in the city to make house calls—perhaps you know him?"

I didn't, so Austin allowed a brief sigh to punctuate his account.

"I don't want to put myself through that prolonged torture. And I certainly don't want to impose such a gruesome experience on Robbie. So I asked Dr. Patel if he had another way. Long story short, Hippocratic oath notwithstanding, the good doctor has devised a lovely cocktail of drugs he claims will do away with me in no time flat whenever I am ready."

"What does Robbie say about this plan?"

"At first he was against it. Lots of wailing and rending of garments, like in some kind of Greek tragedy. He always tries to stomp on my fun, doesn't he? But after more phone and e-mail exchanges with Dr. Patel, he has come around to it in these last few days."

Austin paused to consider the next chapter of his account.

"You know, if I am going to tell you the rest of this story, I will need more sweets. Please bring out the entire cake, Mr. Ryder, and we will fortify ourselves in good fashion. More milk too, if you please."

I followed orders silently and returned to the library with the still massive cake on its stand, a knife, and the carton of milk. The cats, who had followed me into the kitchen with great hope, settled on the sofa once again and resigned themselves to more conversation.

After eating a second piece of cake, Austin leaped back into the narrative in full stride like the star sprinter he once had been.

"I have found the perfect spot for it. My idea is to take Patel's delicious cocktail some evening soon, and with Robbie's help make my way to St. Nicholas Park. There is a spectacular outcropping of Manhattan schist near the center of the park. I will have Robbie deposit me on a bench in front of the rock formation, and I can just drift off during the night.

"I have enjoyed a marvelous life, Mr. Ryder, and an equally fine death. Now it is time to move on to the next adventure."

I felt anxious, like I had to do something—anything—to intervene.

"It won't work, Mr. Austin. Someone will find you. They will identify you, and Robbie will be in trouble with the law. Your plan has some major holes in it."

I knew I sounded like a coconspirator, and I decided I didn't mind the comparison.

"Well then, help me, Mr. Ryder. Since you seem to be some sort of private investigator, you must have mastered all the other dark arts that accompany that kind of violent career. So now you can give me some professional counsel on how to prevent the calamities you have foreseen."

I was glad that Brina wasn't there to hear this part of the conversation as I plunged ahead with more enthusiasm than I had anticipated. I did understand far more about the grisly aspects of death, disposal, and disappearance than I wanted her to know.

"You can be identified by your teeth and by your fingerprints. So you have to get rid of those."

Austin tapped the bright white incisor on his left side. Then he popped out the dentures and returned them quickly to his mouth.

"The orthodontist who crafted these, Dr. Rogers, bless his soul, died along with his records in an office fire over thirty years ago. No chance of identifying these.

"Fingerprints, now, are a bit more difficult to deal with. Do you have any practical suggestions?"

I did. I described a mixture of caustic acids that, when painted on the fingertips, would blur and eventually erase the identifying whorls.

"It will hurt, you know. Not just sting. Really burn. But you have to let those acids sit on your fingers long enough to completely get rid of the prints."

Austin held out his long hands in front of him chest high, slowly rotating them so that the tobacco-brown palms faced up.

"My dear, I stopped playing piano about five years ago because I could not feel the keys. Such a hard thing to give up. My grandmother Althea taught me to play when I was four, and even after all these years, I felt like I was disappointing her when I stopped.

"So I don't believe a little thing like an acid burn will be much of a problem at all at this point."

We talked on until dusk.

At first, we continued in the established pattern: Austin spoke expansively; I responded in monosyllables. But gradually the structure reversed itself. I found I had stories and images I wanted to share with this strange old man. Experiences and losses I kept buried under a mound of banter, hidden from everyone, even Brina.

I felt an urgency to keep talking, to keep Austin in my grasp a few hours more.

I expected my host's energy or attention to flag as the day faded, but neither did. The man must have been a champion workhorse in his first century.

Just before nightfall, the front door opened, and Austin's companion appeared at last, lugging several burlap bags filled with groceries.

A pale, potbellied man with tufts of sandy hair above each ear and across the top of his head, Robbie Unger was certainly surprised to find a stranger being entertained in his home for the first time in over twenty-five years.

After quick introductions were accomplished, I retreated to the bathroom to allow the two men a private moment for explanatory conversation.

I checked the cell, noting several texts and a missed phone call from Brina. What could I tell her about this remarkable client? How could I explain this extraordinary afternoon and the way Andrew Austin had split me like a can opener? Lacking an immediate answer, I just stowed the darkened phone in my pocket.

When I returned to the kitchen, I found the two partners standing side by side shelving the groceries Robbie had purchased.

I wanted to slip away, but I had a final request of the old man.

"Before you...I mean before too long, I'd like to bring a friend to meet you. Sabrina would love it, I'm sure. If you could give us the time, we'd come whenever it's convenient for you."

Austin grinned broadly.

"I have all the time in the world, Mr. Ryder, all the time in the world now."

———

I brought Brina to see Andrew Austin the following Sunday afternoon.

In honor of the visit, she wore a dress for the first time since I had met her. Brina's regular uniform of flowered blouses and worn jeans suited her casual sexy air. I had never cared much about what she wore, but now I found I liked this dress, with its folds of coral lace floating softly around her legs.

This time Austin's caftan was a simple blue-and-white stripe with orange embroidery framing the neck.

As I had imagined, the old man charmed Brina, astounded her, and made her cry several times over the course of the lively afternoon. Austin had baked a devil's food layer cake and a frothy lemon meringue pie for the occasion. He said that he had wanted to make an angel food cake too, but the symbolism was so unbearably obvious he resisted.

The cats made their appearance early: Brick AKA Peaches, inspected Brina with disdain, and Maggie worked her seductive stylings on me once again. After a brief encounter, the animals departed, leaving the humans to their mysterious communing. Robbie was absent on his errands as was his Sunday habit.

Brina knew every one of the names Austin mentioned and spurred the conversation with questions or detailed observations that made our host's eyes widen in disbelief or admiration. I was content to sit in silence watching the two of them talk on deep into the afternoon.

At her insistence, Austin drew from the library shelves several slim volumes of his own poetry. Bound in sober navy-blue cloth, he called them love poems, so I thought they would be of the flowery romantic variety.

Instead our host regaled us with verse after verse of sexual descriptions, some shimmering with elegant heat, some fond and humorous, others extravagantly rude and designed to shock.

"I gave up being polite when I turned seventy," Austin explained cheerfully. "It seemed like such a huge waste of energy."

The poetry was arrestingly beautiful and erotic. As they read out loud, Brina and Austin laughed, looking at each other and then at me. I sensed the heat rising from my neck to my face and assumed my ears had turned red. I thought they must be laughing at me from some secret place only they could inhabit.

But as they continued laughing, I felt as if they had entered a glamorous conspiracy, and I saw that their glances invited me to join in the fun too.

On and on the bawdy words flowed in the old man's clear tenor voice. After the climax of the third poem on orgasms, I began to laugh. The melancholy, the elation, the plain craziness of the day swept through me, washing away my shyness.

This burst of laughter felt good—strange for sure—but so good.

I knew Austin felt the giddy enchantment too when he invited us to the front parlor and insisted on playing a round of Scott Joplin rags on the neglected grand piano.

I sat next to Brina on the white folding chairs. As we listened to the rollicking concert, she took my hand and squeezed it.

The jaunty music, the piano player's thumping foot taps, the press of her hand against mine, the amber and fig scents from her throat blending with vanilla from her hair—these simple sensations surged inside me, intertwined in a knot of longing and contentment. I felt filled up—completed and absolved of duty the way I felt at the end of a job well done.

When it was finally time to go, we three allies paused one last time in the gathering shadows at the scarlet door. Austin enfolded Brina in his long arms for a moment and kissed her brow.

Lifting his head above her springy curls, the old man caught my eye and winked.

From the gray stone apartment building, I led Brina the three blocks to St. Nicholas Park. There we wandered through the cool lanes until we found the rock formation Austin had called Manhattan schist. The outcropping rose more than twenty feet above its bed of moss and discarded leaves, the irregular surfaces glinting dully in the fading twilight.

We sat in silence for a long time on the bench opposite the massive boulder, holding hands. When the sun set, Brina led me to her apartment. I had never been there before, but its decor didn't capture my attention that night—lots of ferns and philodendrons, faded blue and turquoise in the old oriental rug, stacks of books on the floor, but I wasn't paying much attention.

I was intent on one thing: Kissing her felt right, holding her in my arms felt right, and pressing into her sweet body felt right. Her tangled hair fluttering against my chest and face. Her murmurs gliding into my mind, a balm to soothe the rough edges there. Her golden legs enfolding me, her lips accepting me—it all felt so right.

Two days later, Robbie called me to say that Austin had passed away quietly in the park, precisely as planned.

Chapter 7
THE TRANSPARENT THREAT

"The only thing keeping me from the fiery pit is Sabrina. You hurt her, and I will drag you—bone, flesh, and soul—down into that pit with me. You understand?"

Chapter 8
THE BLUE TUNIC

"Archie Lin says he's got another beef with you."

I had just squished onto the fawn-colored carpet in the agency's front suite when Brina's icy words pinned me to the spot. She'd been able to arrest me like that since day one, but our new entanglement made her far harder to resist and even more delicious to succumb to. I was sprung beyond rescue, and I didn't mind a bit.

As she pointed toward the closed door of my office, Brina sounded pissed at Lin, maybe even at me a little. The glow of our previous night together seemed to have evaporated with the dawn of this new day. The unexpected arrival of the detective harshed her morning mellow just as it was getting started. I couldn't blame her. I shared her distaste for dealing with the cops too often: even when Archibald Lin was doing you a favor, it still felt like a menace wrapped up inside a dubious blessing.

To demonstrate I wasn't spooked by the unwelcome visitor, I shrugged just enough to send coffee sloshing toward the lip of the paper cup I was carrying. Brina's eyes widened at the impending mess, but when I safely landed the offering on the blotter in front of her, her expression softened. The Ethiopian Highland java worked its magic: she inhaled; I exhaled. A smile curled the corner of her mouth, and my innocence was affirmed for at least a few minutes more. I wanted to lean over the desk to steal a quick kiss, but I thought better of the idea. Only a few weeks in, we were still new at this relationship, and maybe the office wasn't the best place to show it off just yet.

I threw back my office door to cause a racket, but the detective lounging on the leather sofa opposite my desk didn't flinch. Archibald Lin was eyeing the combination lock that secured my file cabinets.

"A scrub like you can't possibly have any information of real value, Rook."

A new buzz cut revealed the waxy surface of Lin's scalp in an unbecoming way. Below it his flat moon face was punctuated by the beginnings of a moustache that someone must have told him was going to be rakish when it grew in. The black bristles twitching around his mouth as he talked mesmerized me.

"So why do you insist on keeping those file cabinets under such tight protection? Makes me wonder what secrets you want to keep from the rest of the world."

He grinned as if we were pals, which perhaps he imagined we were.

"Lin, the day my secrets become yours, just buckle on the straitjacket and cart me off to Bellevue."

He shrugged, which reminded me of the coffee I had surrendered a few minutes ago.

"Sabrina says you're pissed at me. Or did she just misread you?"

I leaned back against the edge of my desk to avoid taking a seat behind it and inviting the cop to linger.

"That your subtle way of calling me inscrutable? Again? I don't appreciate the stereotyping, Rook." Lin laughed so I knew he meant the warning.

"Well, as a taxpayer, I don't appreciate you chewing up NYPD payroll loafing in my office when you should be out stealing apples or lifting doughnuts or whatever it is you do instead of serving and protecting."

"Oh. Um. Ouch." He halted his eyes in midroll and closed them instead, as if looking at me caused pain.

"If it wasn't for the clichés, Rook, you wouldn't have a thought in your head, would you?"

I pried my ass from the desk and headed for the door to end this interview. But Archie straightened his bulk on the sofa and tossed out a roadblock.

"I *did* come here with a couple of questions for you, if you can make time in your oh-so-busy schedule."

"Yeah, I'm listening."

"You lose a dead body a few weeks ago?"

I had a fair idea where this was going, but I refused to play along.

"Is that the opium talking, Archie?"

"Old man. I mean, *real* old. Dressed like British royalty and propped on a bench in St. Nicholas Park like he was sitting on a throne addressing parliament."

"I don't know where you get the good stuff, but you're definitely hallucinating now."

Lin plowed on, getting his story out in one long blow.

"The sun, ice, and *rigor mortis* didn't make him pretty. But facial recognition apps work miracles these days. Pictures of the stiff matched up with file photos of Andrew Austin. You know, the old civil rights leader. That geezer died decades ago according to the obits. But yet here he was sitting up dead in the park just as good as new."

"So what's any of this have to do with me?"

I just hoped Lin hadn't had the sense to ask Brina about this. Her transparent face would have given away everything in an instant.

"We questioned Austin's flighty old bag of a partner, and he pointed a well-manicured fingernail at you."

I decided that without truth on my side, scoffing was the strongest defense.

"I've heard about cold cases, but this one beats all. The old man is dead, just plain dead. No sign of foul play..."

"How do you know there's no foul play? I didn't tell you the cause of death."

Smugness delivered with a snarl always worked well against Lin, and I used it here on full blast:

"Because I *know* you, Archie. If you had even one shred of actual evidence to pin on me, you'd have been gloating about it already. But you got exactly *nothing*. Except a frozen corpse, a clueless old widower in mourning, and a digital trail heading nowhere."

At this the detective drooped a bit, his spine curving forward under the oversized shoulder pads that held up his dark suit. I could see drops of sweat skidding down his nape and disappearing under the shirt's wilted collar. This was not how Archie Lin had planned to start his day.

But after a moment of contemplating the actual dead end he had run against, Lin rallied as the bright light of another idea seemed to waft across his face.

"Say, Rook, you don't look like you have anything better to do right now."

He glanced at the bare plateau of my desk and grinned like a snake again.

"So why don't you come with me? I have an appointment with the ladies at the Nu-Wave Loc-ateria to get my hair cornrowed this morning!"

I kept quiet as we drove the five blocks to the gritty corner where the Nu-Wave salon squatted.

I didn't want to let Lin know I was familiar with the beauty parlor, not before I learned what his real business was there. Knowing him, he could be working an informant's tip, busting a drug deal, or looking to score a date for Saturday night.

I had stopped at the shop several times to pick up Brina after one of her marathon sessions of hair crafting and Olympic-sized gossiping. She kept her hair loose most of the time in a billowing statement that seemed to have its own agenda and zip code. But every few weeks she would get the urge to try out a new braided style, and she swore the straight-from-the-Continent specialists at Nu-Wave Loc-ateria were the best in the borough.

For these determined women from Senegal, Ghana, Nigeria, and elsewhere, the specter of Old World poverty drove their creativity and desperation in the new. Brina admired all the Nu-Wave immigrants for their cultural authenticity and race-proud gumption. But above the others, she favored one young stylist from Mali, Aminata Coulibaly. She said Amie kept her looking "on point," which I suppose meant smart, complicated, and beautiful beyond measure.

I didn't know anything about fashion or political statements; I just liked the nubby texture of Brina's braid-covered head under my hands and the way her free-swinging plaits tickled the hair on my chest. So if she wanted to devote large chunks of time and money to Nu-Wave Loc-ateria, I was more than happy to go along.

During those long hours spent under Amie's painstaking care, Brina had learned some of the girl's brief life story. Twenty years old, she had arrived in Harlem only fifteen months ago, the first in her family to make the daunting trip.

She braided hair seven hours a day six days a week in the Nu-Wave, just a few blocks from her apartment. When she wasn't in night classes studying to be an interpreter, Amie cleaned houses to make enough off-the-books cash to pay her rent.

Like the seasoned authoritarian that he was, Archie Lin appropriated a blocked parking spot in a delivery zone in front of the comic book store two doors down from the Nu-Wave. I followed him into the shop, staying a few paces behind to better gauge the reception he would receive there.

The beauty salon was like others of its kind—narrow and shiny with lots of stainless steel fixtures and black laminate countertops worn at the edges. A jumble of combs, picks, brushes, and hairpins nestled among huge jars of pastes, butters, and pomades. Bottles of golden oils flanked tiny flasks of essential fragrances; disembodied sheaves of long black hair lay strewn across the counters. A rack of dangling earrings and another with bottles of nail polish dressed up an unoccupied station near the front of the room. A shiny-faced boy in a miniature dashiki scampered in constant motion sweeping debris from the linoleum floor while bouncy Ghanaian high-life music filled the air.

As I stepped around the wire trellis that fenced off the reception area, I could smell the giant pot of peanut stew that I knew perpetually bubbled in a makeshift kitchen in the back.

This was my third visit to Nu-Wave. On my second, I had waited over thirty minutes for Amie to finish Brina's hairdo. So I had had plenty of time for the Loc-ateria ladies to initiate me into the joys of the enticing *fufu* they cooked in their illegal kitchen. After only a few tries, I had mastered the technique of scooping the gummy paste with two fingers, dipping the morsel in the fragrant soup, and swallowing it in a single motion. No chewing allowed. The applause I earned from the assembled beauticians and customers warmed me as much as the spicy peanut concoction. I hadn't thought this slippery cultural-exchange opportunity would bring me such admiration or that *fufu* could be such an effective aphrodisiac, but it seemed to work that way for Brina later that memorable evening.

Even though I wasn't a complete newcomer, I still felt Archie and I looked out of place as we cruised into the shop—two sweaty male interlopers with short black hair and pale faces.

Twelve beauticians were arrayed in parallel lines along the edges of the shop. Before them in black chairs, clients swiveled in sullen displeasure at our interruption, their impassive dark faces topped by tufts of hair sprouting from half-done coils.

All eyes turned to Archie.

"Ladies, Adowa in the house?"

He was asking for the salon owner, a tiny Ghanaian woman of formidable character whom I had met just once. Although Archie accompanied this inquiry with the broadest smile possible, the beauticians responded with stony silence.

I coughed, hoping to give the cop an unspoken clue on etiquette before we both ended up scalped.

Miraculously, Archie got my hint and revised his opening. He spread his hands wide, looked up and down both rows and started again.

"Pardon me, ladies. No breakfast has made me misplace my manners." Backtracking with a wheedling tone looked good on Archie.

"I meant to say good morning. How are you all?"

Several of the younger stylists murmured a return greeting while their elders held firm.

"Are your families prospering? And your business is doing well, I hope?" The rote phrases elicited more faint responses from the disapproving chorus.

"I wonder if you can tell me where I might find Ms. Adowa this morning?"

Two women standing nearest to the kitchen pointed toward the beaded curtain that dangled in the doorway.

Archie plunged through the swinging drape in search of his contact. I had seen Adowa a few times, and I thought she was tough enough to be a confidential informant and handsome enough to be a date; I suspected she was smart enough to be neither.

But before I could find out more about Lin's business at the Nu-Wave Loc-ateria, I was intercepted by Brina's stylist, Amie Coulibaly, who stepped into my path and beckoned me with a tiny flutter of her hand.

"Please, may I speak with you, Mr. Rook?"

Amie's voice was tremulous and low, her liquid eyes starting from her face under faintly etched brows.

She led me toward the twin black washbasins that crowded the rear of the salon and turned her back to her colleagues in the front of the shop. Amie was slender and tall enough to almost look me in the eye, although politeness kept her gaze focused on the corner wastebasket as she resumed her whispering.

"I need your help, Mr. Rook."

Amie bit her lower lip in a gesture that would have been laughably trite if her trembling had not been so real.

"You—you are the only one who can save me. I beg you, please."

She was frightened, and the tears hovering on her lower lids told me she might collapse into hysteria before she could utter another sentence.

I pulled from my breast pocket a Ross Agency business card.

"Can you get to this address in one hour?"

Amie nodded and curved her fingers around the card, bending it in half.

———

Walking wasn't my strong suit, but I couldn't find Archie Lin anywhere, so I limped the five blocks back to the agency on my own.

Brina was seated at the front desk when I huffed into the suite; crumpled tin foil meant she had just finished her lunch. Hummus wrap with a chaser of Famous Amos chocolate chip cookies. The tang of hot sauce pinged in the air, and suddenly I wanted to taste those spicy sweet traces on her tongue.

Moisture gathered in my mouth in involuntary readiness, eternal hope bubbled into an erotic ache low in my belly, but I decided to stay mum until I cooled down.

Brina looked up at me with narrowed eyes as if reading my mind. Running a hand over her mouth to brush away any crumbs, she tipped her head back to take a sip from a bottle of spring water. Admiring her glorious throat and the elongated triangle of brown skin at her shirt collar gave me a much-needed moment to catch my breath. Winded or not, I wanted to enlist her help fast.

"I need you to join me for a chat with your friend Amie, the beautician."

"Chat? What kind of chat?"

"I don't know exactly. Only that she's in some kind of trouble and thinks I can help her out of it. She's due here any minute."

"I haven't seen her in a few weeks." A hand patted the bouffant outline of her hair. "I feel kind of guilty actually. Did she ask for me?"

"Not directly. But I figure the conversation will go better with you in the lead. Amie sounded spooked, scared even."

Brina nodded, a frown puckering the broad space between her eyes.

"If Amie's in a bad fix, we'll get to the bottom of it. She's a good kid."

———

It turned out Amie Coulibaly's fix was worse than bad.

Once she had settled beside Brina on the couch in front of my desk, Amie poured out her story in a rush of words and sighs. I didn't want to interrupt the torrent, so I watched in silence, leaning back in my chair to make myself as unobtrusive as a six-foot-tall man can be.

The two women were evenly matched in height and shape, both slender and long limbed, with the Sahelian blue-black skin offering a delightful contrast to Brina's burnished bronze.

Amie's long spray of microbraids was arranged in a careful cascade over her right shoulder, a white ribbon gathering the strands like a sheaf of black wheat.

When I'd met her in the beauty shop, she'd been wearing a loose black T-shirt and jeans under a yellow cloth apron, but now her slim body was swaddled in yards of blue and white tie-dyed fabric. Underneath her tunic she wore a navy-blue turtleneck to ward off the American winter.

Her dark almond-shaped eyes started from her face under eyelashes that were heavy and silky as a doe's. Unlike Brina's luxuriant eyebrows, Amie had only a faint scattering of hairs arranged in a sculpted arc to punctuate the smooth dome of her forehead.

Trembling lips and her lilting English made Amie's story hard to follow. Or perhaps it was the fear that jumbled her phrases and boxed her words. She sketched out an immigrant's tale that filled in our understanding of her tense profile.

Amie had arrived in the United States three years ago, her trip a fishing expedition financed by her much-older husband. Alhajii Hassan Bah was a big man in their village, but he had ambitions of establishing a beachhead in New York City. A pliant wife working at a lucrative job could be converted into a successful visa application for many members of his extended family. At least that was the plan, as Amie understood it.

She easily found employment as a braider of hair. She was hardly the best stylist back home, so it seemed ridiculous to her that a common skill easily mastered by every small girl in her village could command such high prices from black women on this side of the Atlantic. She wondered if American mothers neglected to teach their daughters other essential lessons of femininity and domestic crafts. But arguing with good luck was not Amie's style. She just worked hard and marveled at how the cash flowed in each month. She stored her savings from Nu-Wave in glass jars under her bed. She worked six days a week, ten hours each day; after much palaver, she won permission to break at three on Fridays to attend prayer services and then rest at home on Sundays when the Christians took their holiday. Resplendent in their bottles, the thick rolls of green dollars represented her future and that of her entire family.

But Amie's joy was interrupted four months ago when her husband's younger brother arrived in the United States to stay with her. Boubacar Bah didn't have a regular job and contributed little to her rent. Once in a while, he received a box of leather and bead trinkets from his brother, which he sold at a curbside table he shared with another Malian immigrant. After only a few weeks in the United States, Boubacar got into a horrible argument with the three men who rented the rooms opposite Amie's apartment. Amie claimed she knew little about her neighbors, only that they were also West Africans, Bambara from Mali too. She was glad these men were quiet like she was, friendly and proper, but they had no known employment that she could tell.

"But what's the danger, Amie? What do you fear so much?" Brina kept her voice low to limit the stress, but her direct questions were designed to propel Amie's roundabout narrative style. I was glad that I had asked Brina to join the conversation as I didn't think my clumsy male intervention would be appreciated.

Amie resumed her story, this time with a noticeable hesitation between words. "Last night, the arguments became even worse. Boubacar accused the men of terrible things..." Here Amie trailed off again and hiccupped over a sob.

"But what terrible things did they do? You have to tell us Amie, if you want us to help you." I could tell Brina was getting both anxious and impatient, but I admired the way she kept most of those emotions out of her voice.

Amie bit her lip again and twisted her fingers, picking at the cuticles until raw pink edges appeared beside several nails. She curved an arm around her waist and doubled over in what looked like pain.

"I don't know how to say it, Brina. It's too awful."

"Just say it, and we'll go from there. Nothing is too awful between friends." Brina placed an arm over Amie's shuddering back, gently urging her on.

"During the months I was here, before Boubacar arrived, I wasn't alone, not completely…"

"Did you have a boyfriend, Amie? Is that what it is?"

"Yes, a boyfriend. One of my neighbors became my boyfriend. Ahmed was kind to me—generous and gentle and patient with me. He became my friend and then we…well, we acted as husband and wife."

Amie sobbed once, but having aired the worst of her story, she resumed at a more rapid pace.

"I knew it was wrong. But I was lonely. I never thought anyone from home would ever know. It's so easy for you American girls here. I watch you all the time. You all have boyfriends and husbands and no one seems to mind how many you go with. But for us it is not the same."

Without challenging Amie's assumptions about American morality, Brina jumped ahead to the story's difficult conclusion. "So everything was OK until your husband's brother Boubacar arrived. That upset everything, didn't it?"

"Yes, it did. But things still might have been all right. Ahmed and I agreed to separate. It was hard because he lives just across the hall from me. But we were good and stayed apart. But then three weeks ago, I found out I am expecting a baby. Ahmed's baby."

Amie's eyes bulged from her head at the horror of her predicament. Tears coursed down her cheeks, dripping from her chin onto the blue tunic that disguised her condition.

"Last night, Boubacar overheard me speaking with Ahmed, and he learned all. I am afraid to go home now. I am lost. Nothing can ever put it right again. I am lost. Lost."

As Brina patted her shoulder and touched little kisses to her forehead, Amie let out a piteous wail. I couldn't stand to witness her misery, so I made myself useful by retreating to the bathroom for a stack of paper towels and a glass of cool water. I left these meager offerings on my desk and went to sit in Brina's chair out front. I would leave the women alone to reach any decisions about Amie's situation. They were smart, level headed, and practical; I trusted the solution they found would be just fine.

So I was bowled over when the two women emerged from my office twenty minutes later with their fierce eyes fixed on me. It turned out I was their solution.

Holding her friend's hand, Brina explained my role.

"I've told Amie she can stay with me for a few days. But you've got to go with Amie to her apartment to help collect her belongings. All those men—her brother-in-law, her boyfriend and his pals—could be around, putting Amie in danger. So I've told her you'll be her escort and her protection. Who knows? Maybe you can even get them to sit down together, talk man to man. You know, get them to start thinking about the future instead of acting like fool lions in a Nat Geo special or something."

I didn't have a lot of confidence in my negotiating skills in this delicate situation. There were too many unknown variables, and I was no ambassador. But I got Brina's point about needing to assert a diplomatic presence, a male approach. Maybe I could be effective as the neutral observer arranging a peace treaty between the brother-in-law and the boyfriend. I liked that image of me as a striped-pants-wearing attaché. It was a lot better than Brina's vision of me as a big game hunter in khaki shorts caught between two charging lions.

———

But when we got to Amie's place, the scene was far different from what I had imagined. Horrific, in fact.

Her apartment was crawling with cops, in uniform and plain clothes. The door was already ajar, so we stepped inside unannounced and surveyed the scene. A body lay in the middle of the living room, covered in a shroud of thin blue fabric. The shoes told me it was a man, but with the face hidden, there was no way to know who it was. Bright red staining the tunic just below the chin suggested that a slashed throat was the cause of death.

A dozen technicians in navy windbreakers scurried about the apartment, too busy with the minutiae of their work to notice us transfixed in the entrance. They swept up microscopic shards of glass, shorn nails, motes of dust, flakes of discarded skin, and fibers shed from the dead man's clothing, hoping to find the damning sliver of evidence that would convict his murderer. Crouching, crawling, they plucked and picked until they had filled a hundred plastic envelopes with the sad treasures of their hunt.

Amie trembled at my side, her vibrations violent enough to send her crashing into me. Before she could hit the floor, I caught her and squeezed her against my chest. I looked around for the officer in charge, but there seemed to be no one directing the murder investigation.

At a glance, I took in the bare details of Amie's apartment and the aspirations it revealed. The space was narrow, but the corners were swept clean around the edges of the dingy parlor carpet. Every wall was painted in noncommittal shades of vanilla, the landlord's drab touch, no doubt.

But Amie had tacked stunning cloths in bright primary stripes on all four walls of her living room. Another long swath of colorful fabric was festooned along the grimy corridor wall leading toward the rear of the apartment.

Loud reds and yellows, black, white, and green predominated, with bold fringe draping down from the ends of each textile like braided coils from a woman's head.

Amie had been an optimistic decorator when she first arrived in America, determined to display these tokens of home, pride, and hope where she could treasure them every day. Now all optimism was dashed, murdered along with the man under that blue tunic.

"How'd you get in here?"

The bark caused Amie to jerk in the circle of my arms. She started to moan, a sound more like a growl than a cry.

I answered for her. "Officer, this woman lives here. It's her apartment. Can you tell us what happened here?"

I hoped that by keeping my voice even and as mild as I could, the cop would answer in kind. But he didn't bother to moderate the harshness of his reply.

"You can see for yourself what happened, can't you? Somebody slashed that guy's throat and left him to bleed out in the middle of her living room." At that, Amie lunged forward, reaching out to touch the body on the floor. She wanted to see which of her loved ones was dead and which was guilty. I held her by both arms until she stopped struggling.

"Tell me!" The guttural sound rasped from her throat like the howl of an animal trapped in a deep well. "Tell me who it is!"

Before the abrupt cop could reply, another officer stepped in front of us. His voice was deep, authoritative.

"You don't need to see this, Miss. Please let Detective Thomas take you back to the kitchen. You can wait for us there." With a commanding tip of his chin, he signaled to a female officer who gripped Amie's elbow to steer her down the hall, away from the gruesome scene. I stayed behind. Watching Amie disappear into the kitchen, a surge of gratitude made my head swim.

"Thank you, officer. I appreciate you stepping in like that."

Turning back to look at the man who had rescued Amie, I was knocked back by the tap of uneasy recognition. Sinewy and hunched beneath his oversized uniform, Officer Nelson studied me with huge eyes. Our curb-side interview on the night of the Rouge fire had been fleeting but memorable. He recognized me too.

"Rook, isn't it? You look a lot better now than when I saw you over at the Rouge. What are you doing here? You know this girl?"

His voice stayed even, but I thought I heard a whisper of tension beneath the formal demeanor. I sketched my connection to Amie Coulibaly without volunteering any personal details about Amie, her brother-in-law, or her lover. I wasn't going to do his job for him.

"So you her lawyer or something? 'Cause she's going to need one. That poor bastard under the sheet over there had a passport on him said he was from Africa or somewhere. If she's related to him, then I guess she's from over there too."

"She didn't kill him. You could see for yourself she was in shock when we walked in the room."

"Yeah, I figured that out for myself. Anyway, we already shipped off another one of them down to the precinct. From Africa, too, by the looks of him. We figure him for the perp. He was still holding a giant curved blade, sitting over there on that couch, just as quiet as you please when police got here. The super called us cause of all the ruckus, but by the time we arrived on the scene, the place was quiet. The dead man was wrapped up like a pretty package in that blue tunic. And the other one was just slumped on the sofa, staring at the sword in his hand like he never seen it before. Don't that just beat all? I figure they fought over the girl, right? Bitch is always at the center of it. Every time, it's the bitch. Count on it."

Cynical and caustic, Nelson's summary left unclear who had died and who lived. Poor Amie would have to make the identification herself to end the mystery.

"So like I said, you her lawyer? I already put in a call to ICE. If even one comma is out of place on their immigration papers, those ICE boys'll ship the whole lot of 'em back to the jungle."

"They're from the Sahara Desert. And I'm not a lawyer. I'm a private investigator."

The new title slipped over my tongue with ease, no hitch or stutter. It felt right, like it fit me. I gave Nelson a Ross Agency card. He glanced at it and then stuck it between the leaves of his notebook with a grunt.

"Private eye, huh? Well, I don't care whether the bitch's from the desert or the jungle or the fuckin' Taj Mahal. She's gonna need a lawyer, and she's gonna need one fast."

With that, our second interview ended as abruptly as it had begun. Nelson turned his back on me and trotted down the hall to the kitchen to question Amie.

I wanted to stay around until I knew something more of her fate. I couldn't help her perhaps, but at least I could serve as a sympathetic witness. After forty minutes, Nelson brought Amie to the front parlor to make the identification. He pulled the blue tunic back so that only the forehead and eyes of the dead man were revealed. She said one name, "Boubacar," and then collapsed onto the sofa. Before she hid her face behind quivering hands, I thought a faint smile flickered across her lips, but I couldn't be sure.

After a few minutes, Officer Thomas escorted Amie from the building, taking her into protective custody as a material witness in the murder investigation. I never saw her again.

With her departure, my work was over; the Ross Agency file on Aminata Coulibaly closed. As I walked back to the office, the day's burden of grief pressed down on me. I felt exhausted, dirty, and nauseous. I hoped Brina wasn't waiting for me because I dreaded telling her how this case had ended. She wasn't, and I gave thanks for that temporary reprieve.

Chapter 9

THE GREEN TEA CURE

A vicious flu bug laid me up for four days after Aminata Coulibaly was incarcerated in the federal immigration detention center in Newark.

I don't know if my immune system was damaged in the aftermath of that dismal case or if I'd been exposed to some toxic virus weeks ago. But whatever it was, it hit me like a sixteen-wheeler with busted brakes. For days I lay flat on my back on the office sofa, buried under a green blanket Brina donated and a garish plaid topcoat Norment Ross dragged from the back of his closet.

"I thought you said it was just a twenty-four-hour bug." I detected a hint of complaint in Brina's soft voice. "At least, that's what you told me seventy-two hours ago."

She had offered to put me up at her apartment when I first fell ill. But the prospect of Brina seeing me at my weakest seemed far worse than the disease itself. I didn't want her to nurse or coddle or pity me. An affair with the boss's daughter was dicey enough without adding sick room vulnerabilities to the mix, so I declined the suggestion.

I hoped to counter her frustration. "Yeah, well, I guess that medical degree I got online wasn't so good after all." But the racking cough that punctuated my quip underlined its weakness and made her frown. She was winding up to deliver another Florence Nightingale scolding when Ross burst through the door, a jar of fluorescent green fluid in his hand.

"Mei Young sent you some of her special green tea. This stuff here'll cure you of whatever ails you, believe you me."

Ross set the quart jar on the floor next to the sofa and took a seat behind my desk. I appreciated the chicken broth Mei Young had supplied twice daily for the past half week; it was the only thing my troubled stomach could keep down. But I was skeptical about this swirling brew Ross had brought. I guess the doubt showed on my face because Ross then launched into a full-throated sales pitch for the restorative qualities of Mei Young's green tea.

"I take it to cure hangovers, colds, the trots, everything. I'm telling you, Mei knows what she's doing. When my arthritis kicks up bad, a cup of this tea knocks down the pain faster than you can say Jack Robinson."

He stared at Brina for confirmation of the brew's wondrous properties.

"Remember when I got that bout of the shingles—ugly red lizard scales all around my waist and up and down my back like you wouldn't believe. A couple quarts of this green tea fixed me up good. Right as rain. Remember, Brina?"

We both looked at Brina to see if she would contradict her father's medical history. A wise daughter, she just shrugged and passed her long cool fingers over my forehead.

"Look. It won't hurt you; that's for sure. You need to keep taking fluids, and this tea is a good way to do it."

She picked up the jar and held it to my lips. I propped myself up on my elbows and took a sip. The lukewarm tea tasted grassy and clean. I liked the top note of sweetness and the kick of spice that followed. I also liked the intimacy of having Brina take care of me in front of her father this way. This seemed like a new step for us, one I hoped we could push further as time went along. I wasn't sure Mei Young's green tea would cure me, but it definitely made me feel better.

Brina kissed the top of my head and then left the room. I thought her father would follow; a sick ward was hardly a cheery place to hang out. But he stayed put at my desk, rearranging the pencils and pens into a formation that suited him, pushing the pads of notepaper to one side, and finding a better corner for my coffee mug. I figured Ross had something to say. Since I wasn't going anywhere, I lay still, staring at the ceiling as I let the green tea work its cure. After a few moments of silence, he blurted out his question.

"You ever been to that new night club, the Jumeaux?"

"No. I've heard Brina talk about it. Her friend Pinky sings there, you know. But I haven't gotten there yet. Why?"

"One of those fancy tricked-out Dreyfus twins that owns the place asked me to stop by tonight. Take a look around."

"What for?"

"He said he was having some labor troubles. You know, a personnel dispute. Some kind of ruckus between the service crew and the band. I guess he hoped I could step in and straighten it out."

"What kind of trouble?"

"He only sketched it out for me. He said last night two of his staff got into a tussle in the kitchen. You know: eye scratching, hair pulling, earring snatching. An old-style catfight."

"I don't see how you can help. Why didn't he just fire them all?"

"That's what I said. But he asked as a favor 'cause he knows Brina. So I said I would drop by."

I guessed Ross wanted my help with the case. He could see that I was in no condition to accompany him to the club that evening. But he wanted to pick my brains anyway. My brains were fried by fever, but the mental exercise was welcome after four days of inertia, so I tried out another question.

"Well, who are the combatants?"

"One's a white girl just arrived off the bus from Wisconsin, name Danica. The other's a girl from down the block, name Floretta."

I nodded in understanding and let my fancy fly.

"Hmm, Danica, the farm girl versus Floretta, the home girl. Sounds like a juicy bantamweight match to me. The Dreyfus twins ought to charge admission for the next round."

I smiled up at the ceiling as I imagined this scenario and shifted under the confines of the heavy blanket and overcoat. The chills seeped from my body as the minutes passed, but my feet still felt ice cold. Ross could tell he had captured my attention so he dragged me further into the case with his next question.

"What do you figure is the beef between these two chicks anyway?"

"It must be the bass player. He's the one at fault. You can bet your last dollar on it."

"How in the world do you come up with that?"

He was asking for speculation, so with nothing to lose and nothing to go on, I rolled over on my side to look at him square and swung for the fences.

"Well, here's how it could go. I figure Danica's a runaway. Probably met a cool boy in high school, got hooked up with meth or something harder. Cool Boyfriend persuaded her to quit her boring life in Wisconsin for the bright lights of the big city. When they got here, Cool Boyfriend skipped out, leaving Farm Girl alone and miserable. She found a job waitressing at the nightclub. I bet she's cute, so getting a job like that wasn't too hard. Snap your fingers and boom! She's screwing the bass player. But I figure the bass player isn't exactly at liberty, you know. His other side chick, that's our homegirl Floretta, took exception to the corn-fed Miss Wisconsin, and now Danica's in danger of getting murdered by jealous groupie number one."

The long story had winded me, and I fell back against the pillow, my eyes glued to the ceiling again.

"That's pretty cynical there, Rook. But why blame the bass player?"

"It's always the bass player. In mystery novels, the butler does it. But in real life, it's the bass player. Every time."

I was pulling his leg, but Ross seemed to give my hypothesis real consideration. At least he didn't dismiss it out of hand as I had expected him to.

"Yeah, well, who knows? You could be right. I'll keep an eye out tonight at the club."

I pulled the plaid coat's velvet collar up around my ears and snuggled deeper under the covers. The green tea was making me drowsy, but

I croaked out a weak phrase as Ross closed the door. "Let me know how it turns out, Norment."

———

The next evening, Ross briefed me on his investigations at the Jumeaux nightclub.

"Damned if it didn't turn out just like you said, Rook. The girls were fighting over one of the band members. I told Dreyfus to clean house and fire the lot of 'em. But he took the advice of his band leader instead. He dumped the musician and switched shifts for the two girls. I asked why he handled it like that. He said, 'I can toss a net out on the boulevard and find six new horn players in fifty minutes. But these chicks are good at the job, bringing in good tips, keeping the customers happy. So I need to hang on to them as best I can.'"

Shaking his heavy head, Ross bugged his eyes out in wonder at the fickleness of humanity.

"Don't that just beat all?"

I sat up from my sickbed to hear Ross tell the story, my elbows on my knees, the plaid coat slung over my shoulders. With great effort, I managed to keep a straight face during this account.

"So it turned out it wasn't the bass player after all?"

"No, you got that part wrong, Rook." The grin splitting Ross's face looked broad enough to hurt. "Mr. Slick played the trumpet."

I guess I looked dejected at my misstep, so Ross tried to buck up my spirits.

"Hey, no worries, partner; you were damn good. Lying flat on your back like that, sick as a dog, you figured it out. Mostly. That's a pretty damn fine piece of detecting in my book."

I didn't miss the new title I had earned: "partner." It sounded good.

———

Pork rinds were calling my name. Not the crunchy lime-juice-dipped *chicharrons* that my grandmother used to prepare as family snacks on Sundays. I would never get to taste those deep-fried delicacies again. So now I longed for the commercial pork rinds, packaged in plastic sacks and coated with five-syllable chemical compounds buried in salt. Four days of flu-induced starvation had primed me for any sort of junk food I could get my hands on—the sweeter and greasier the better.

When Ross and Brina left me to my own devices for another night at the office, I took advantage of their absence to plan a sneak sortie to the corner bodega in search of snacks and soft drinks. With Ross's brassy plaid overcoat wrapped around my depleted frame, I crept on shaky legs past the shuttered Korean grocery and the nail salon where a single manicurist tinkered over her last customer. The bodega was still open at ten past eleven. Carlito sold me a week's supply of Ho Hos, Reese's peanut-butter cups, Fritos, Almond Joy bars, Lay's potato chips, SweeTarts, and a bottle of orange Fanta. He was out of pork rinds.

I had made the return trip as far as the Korean storefront when a volley of shots rang out. Two bullets clanked into the grocery's metal shutter at head height, just to my left. Another whizzed past my ear when I crouched. I felt hot pressure on my right arm, which drove me flat to the sidewalk. I heard a car engine rev and shouts from the bar across the street. The few pedestrians on the block had scattered when the gunfire started, but Carlito ran to my side, as did the manicurist. I felt OK—rattled but uninjured—so I shrugged off their help. Despite my bravado, the burly bodega clerk and the tiny manicurist escorted me the rest of the way home. At the door of the Emerald Garden, Carlito handed me the bag of snacks. I was grateful for their attention, but disappointed that they had seen nothing of my assailant.

By the time I made it through the darkened restaurant kitchen and up the stairs, I knew something was wrong with me. My right arm felt heavy, alternately pulsing and stinging in a frantic rhythm. Flicking on the light in my office, I inspected the damage: above the right elbow, the sleeves of Ross's garish overcoat and my shirt bore nasty slashes framed by blackened edges. The three-inch-long gash on my right biceps resembled an angry red trench. No bullet puncture or broken skin but plenty of tenderness and bruising.

Brina kept a rudimentary first-aid kit in the bathroom. I slathered antiseptic ointment over the throbbing crease on my arm. I measured a length of gauze bandage to bind up my injury, but decided against it for the moment. If the damaged muscle continued to hurt through the night, I might construct a sling to support it, but that could wait until morning. Rather than taking aspirin, I decided to kill the escalating pain with a few swigs of bourbon. I kept the bottle in the bottom drawer of my desk, saving it for rare occasions. Getting shot seemed like the perfect occasion.

Though my arm escaped major damage, the orange Fanta bottle had taken a devastating hit. So bourbon was all I had to accompany the stash of sweet and salty junk that comforted me through the night. By the time I finished the second glass, I decided that the drive-by attack might have been aimed at Norment Ross. I knew he had enemies; all those cases over all those years must have resulted in more than a few hard feelings. And as I shared his height and general build, walking down the night street in his ugly plaid overcoat, I might have looked enough like Norment to fool a careless hitman. But the issue of timing threw a dent in that supposition. The Ross Agency had occupied the offices above the Emerald Garden for decades, so anyone with a grudge could find out where Norment Ross operated and take a pot shot at any time. Why wait until tonight to strike?

On the other hand, I had worked just a few cases, none controversial as far as I could see. Unfaithful cats, suicidal old men, jealous immigrants, and rampaging community agitators didn't add up to anyone who'd want to shoot me. After these few months on the job, I knew only a handful of people; did any of them despise me enough to resort to murder?

The bourbon, plus heavy doses of empty calories, cleared my mind, or it turned the sloppy mush clogging my head into an avalanche. Either way, as the night churned on, thoughts kept rushing over one another, jostling and defiant in their desire to be considered.

People got murdered because of just a few fatal bits of information: what or who they knew; what they saw or heard; what they could do or say. Sometimes the victim didn't even know he possessed the deadly fragment of insight. Murder did not take two to tango. Only the killer needed to know that the factoid was important. So the most effective kill, a clean murder, erased the information and the person who held it in a single blow. Did I know too much *and* too little at the same time?

The bourbon required a chaser of tap water, so I got a glassful from the bathroom. When I returned to my office, the mess was daunting: candy wrappers and crumbs littered the floor in front of the couch; the upended bourbon bottle had dribbled an offering to the ancestors onto the dingy carpet. I had stepped on the open potato-chip bag, crushing its contents. But at least the Fritos were intact.

I retrieved the corn chips from the floor and started crunching. The Fritos bag reminded me of the identical one I had seen at the feet of poor departed Larry Sherman a few weeks ago. I knew from Archibald Lin's whining that police remained baffled by that murder. The Worm had no family, no friends, and no mourners to provide leads in the investigation. No business contacts except for a few tenants, an unhappy insurance agent, the lost girls of the Auberge Rouge, and me. But what if Larry and I were linked by stronger chains than that? What if we were manacled together by something we saw, someone we knew, some fragment of fatal information that meant nothing to us and everything to a violent killer?

I scoured my memories of the night of the Rouge fire, but they were still blurred by booze and shock. I remembered the girls in the lobby purring their louche greetings at me as I entered the inn. Larry encased in his Plexiglas cubicle. Two, no three, men heading to the upper floors as I climbed the stairs to my room—one with an eye patch and one with a gold tooth. The third man was only a hunched shadow in the corner of my mind.

I thought about the girls who died on the floors above me. I remembered Colleen, and I wanted to ask Norment Ross a question about her before she became just another lost ghost flickering across my memory.

It was three in the morning, but I made the call anyway.

"Man, what's the matter with you? You know what time it is? Is something wrong with Brina? That's the only reason for you to call me at this hour. Is she OK?"

"Sabrina is fine, Norment. Safe in her own bed." I tried to keep my voice smooth to disguise the panic and the bourbon that coursed through my veins.

"That's right, because decent people asleep at this hour. Only fools like you on the phone. You not drunk dialing, are you? I oughta shoot you where you stand, waking me up like this."

I didn't tell him someone had already beaten him to it. And I didn't confess I was drunk either. I could hear the sleep clearing from his voice as the surprise dissipated.

"I'm sorry for the late call, Norment. But I need some information from you. And it can't wait." I paused to collect my thoughts, and I guess my hesitation extended too long for him.

"So go on with your damn fool question. I ain't got all night."

"Tell me about Colleen McClatchy's john, the bully you scared off a few years back."

"What you want to know about that worthless piece of shit for?"

"I just need to know what he looked like, that's all. Can you describe him to me?"

"I only saw him those two times I roughed him up a bit. But as far as I remember, he was a scrawny little SOB—big old staring eyes, two buck teeth set in a dark face."

"Kinda like a rabbit, would you say?"

"Yeah, sure. If a rabbit was mean, aggressive, and selfish."

Colleen's bully was Nelson the police officer. I had seen him two times after the fire, but also once *before* it. He was the third man on the stairs in the doomed Rouge, I was sure of it now. Like Larry Sherman, I could place Nelson in the brothel before the blaze began. If Nelson was guilty of a crime at the Rouge, we both could identify him. And with Larry dead, I was the only remaining witness.

I thanked Norment for his information and apologized again for the interruption. No need to share my conclusions with him yet. I needed to sober up, nurse my aching arm, and get some rest in the few hours until dawn. I wanted to test the ideas swirling in my scrambled head in the clear light of the new day. We would have time tomorrow to review the case of the Auberge Rouge.

Chapter 10
THE CARBON HEART

The nasty crease on my arm looked worse in stark daylight.

Red, swollen, and jagged, the word "graze" seemed too gentle a term to apply to this damaged flesh. Brina's probing made the wound pulse and burn, but I only squirmed a bit. I felt better for her attention, her kisses, and the tears she shed for me. She brought me three egg sandwiches from the Emerald Garden kitchen, runny the way I like them, which did wonders for my aching arm. And for the huge throbbing crater that had opened up inside my head. I didn't see any need to mention exactly how much bourbon I had consumed after the shooting. If she believed that my morning pain was all due to the bullet's glancing blow, I was happy to let her go with that.

After a few minutes of pleading, Brina accepted my decision to skip the emergency room. And Ross agreed with me that bringing the cops into a fuzzy situation without adequate explanation was a recipe for disaster.

"You don't have any proof of an underlying crime in the Rouge fire, do you?"

I shook my head, a mistake that set my temples screaming again.

"Right. I don't know if Nelson started it or not. I don't know if he harmed Colleen before the fire or not."

"So what you got is a big pile of nothing right now."

Brina, ever the logical one, objected: "You hold back information, and you could end up in jail yourself."

"Give me a day to get proof. If I don't have any concrete evidence by tomorrow morning, then we go to the cops." Brina squinted in skepticism, but Ross nodded his agreement.

"And just how do you propose to get that proof?"

Before I could answer her father, Brina jumped ahead: "You're going to offer yourself up as bait, aren't you? Try to lure Nelson by putting yourself in harm's way. Are you crazy?"

I ignored her last question, figuring she knew the answer to that one by now.

"If I'm right, Nelson knows I saw him at the Rouge. He needs to get rid of me before I put all the pieces together."

"Well, why didn't he come after you before now?"

"I figure he lost track of me after the night of the fire. He interviewed me on the street that night to see how much I remembered. But hungover and dazed like I was, I didn't know much. I think he would have tracked me down after that. But I didn't have a known address, and he couldn't find me. Until I turned up at Amie Coulibaly's apartment and gave him my business card."

Ross chimed in: "Then you took sick with the flu and disappeared for five days. Even Nelson didn't have the brass balls to come up to the agency asking about you. He might have worried I'd recognize him. So he hung around the place, and when you went out last night, he took his opportunity."

"Exactly. Nelson tried once, and he'll try again. Soon."

———

Nelson was watching the Emerald Garden, I was sure of it. But I figured even the most determined assassin would wait until nightfall before launching an attack. So I loitered around the restaurant all day. I ate lunch at a table in the front window. In the afternoon, I left the premises only twice: to pick up dry cleaning from Mrs. Lee next door and a quart of milk from Mr. Oh.

I grew antsy as the hours dragged on. When Rashid, one of Ross's whist buddies, stopped in looking for a game, I persuaded him to sit with me on the patio outside the restaurant for a few rounds of two-handed gin rummy. Bundled up in thick overcoats and wool watch caps against the early December frost, I thought we must look a bizarre sight, even in a neighborhood of eccentrics. As we played, Rashid, who was an attorney, brought me up to date on a recent client, Aminata Coulibaly. Ross had told him of my involvement in her sad case. Rashid reported that Amie had been released from ICE detention and was now waiting to testify in the murder trial of her lover, Ahmed. Their baby, a son, was due in late January. I felt giddy at this news, as if Amie's reprieve was a cheerful omen, a sign that maybe I was on the right track at last. When Rashid left, chilled to the bone but several dollars richer, I returned to my post at the front window of the Emerald Garden.

At dusk, I asked Mei Young to close the restaurant for the evening. I didn't want her or her customers caught in any crossfire. Though I promised to pay her for the lost income, she just snorted in derision. I guess she knew I wasn't good for the money. After she posted the "Closed" sign on the door, Mei shrugged and left me alone in the darkened room.

By plan, Norment and Brina made a show of leaving the building a few minutes later. They shouted out their plans for dinner at the swanky new restaurant, Sugar's, and then perhaps taking in Pinky's nightclub act. They slammed the door so hard the glass rattled in its frame and several pedestrians turned to stare at the disturbance. I stayed behind in the shuttered Emerald Garden. I was the bait, luring the attacker for a second attempt. And the Rosses were the trap.

For three hours in the pitch black, I sat at the table at the rear of the room nearest the kitchen. I wanted as much space as possible between me and the front door to give me time to react to Nelson's expected assault.

This was a fine idea, except he came at me from behind.

I didn't hear anything until Nelson was at my shoulder. His heated breath blew across my cheek, and I felt a swooshing movement as his arm carved a tight circle around my torso. Although I couldn't see it, I knew he had a knife, his preferred weapon. I raised my right arm to block his blow, pushing the chair backward as I rose. When he yelped as the chair thudded against his shin, I turned and powered my left fist into his midsection. Nelson drew the blade across my forearm, the sound like ripping silk from a bolt of fabric. When I staggered, he backed toward the kitchen, waving the knife in a desperate arc. I grabbed the chair and lunged forward, thrusting its legs at his face. Metal clanked against hollow metal as I countered his jabs. The chair wasn't heavy, but my injured right arm ached with the effort of wielding it; I figured I was good for only two or three more swipes before I had to drop my shield. With the second swing, I connected to muscle and then bone. I heard a sharp crack, brittle and close, the way a dry twig sounds when you step on it. Nelson's high squeal masked the clatter of the knife hitting the floor. If he was unarmed, I could tackle him. I stepped forward, but instead of falling, Nelson retreated into the kitchen. I heard wet open-mouthed panting as fingernails scrabbled over the steel countertops in search of another weapon. His back to the sink, he found a row of knives pinned to the wall on a magnetic strip. Again, he raised his arm in an arc; the dagger pointing toward me was longer this time, its reach more accurate.

The bolt of fluorescent light blinded us both.

"Get out of my kitchen!" Mei Young stood in the rear doorway, her hand still on the wall switch, the red silk rope swinging like a pendulum from her waist.

Nelson recovered from the shock first. He turned his blazing eyes on me and lowered the knife to chest height. As he stalked forward, I grabbed an iron skillet, hoping I could swat the weapon from his hand or deflect its thrust. When he was an arm's length from me, a shot rang through the kitchen. Then another. Nelson clutch his left hip, fingers digging into the flesh as if to extract the bullets lodged there. His eyes bulged from his head, and he collapsed to the floor, lips twisted and gaping. I kicked the knife away from his outstretched fingers. As I dropped to my knees beside him, Brina stepped into the kitchen, her gun pointed at the prone man.

"Move again, and I put the next one in your head." At her command, Nelson lay still, moaning like a stunned animal caught in the trap's serrated vise.

Norment Ross flowed into the narrow space, a hand on his holstered gun. He nodded at Mei, then his daughter, and finally at me.

"Everybody all right in here?"

Ross reached for his cell phone, but I stopped him.

"Don't call the medics yet. Or the police. I want a few answers before they come."

"The man is bleeding out, Rook." Brina stared at me with enormous eyes. Her voice shook with horror. "He needs to get to a hospital fast."

I ignored her, keeping my glare on my prey.

"The faster you talk, Nelson, the faster you get help. You understand?"

"I don't know what you want."

"A few simple answers, and I dial nine one one. How long you lie here bleeding depends on you."

"What do you want to know?"

"Did you hurt Colleen McClatchy the night of the Rouge fire?"

"Yeah, I did her." He gasped out the first sentence. But a snarl propelled the next words: "Slit the bitch's throat. Then I set fire to her room."

"Why? Why'd you do that?" Brina's anguish for the lost girl overrode her concern for Nelson's deteriorating condition as she knelt beside him.

With lips drawn back from dark gums, he spit out the answer: "She laughed at me. Bitch wouldn't stop laughing at me."

Silence curled around the four of us as we stared at the stricken man on the floor. Mei Young opened a drawer and threw a pile of dish towels at him. I used them to staunch the blood flowing from wounds at his hip and lower stomach. Brina interrupted me to knot a towel around my bleeding forearm.

"And Larry Sherman? What about him?" I lifted my fist from the towels on Nelson's stomach and watched as the blood flowed again.

"Yeah, him too. He saw me at the Rouge that night. Just like you, he knew it was me. Only when I went to his house, he acted like we were old friends, smiled, and welcomed me in and all. But I stabbed him anyway, just to make sure he didn't talk."

I resumed my pressure on the cop's wounds and nodded at Ross to make the calls. Nelson never lost consciousness as we waited for the ambulance and the police. He never said another word.

Chapter 11
THE GOLDEN PROMISE

"Sabrina loves you, Rook. That's all there is to it. Some kind of fellow feeling between you two, a mix of shared experiences, maybe even common sorrows, that binds you two together. I don't know if either of you get what it is really. But I promise you this: you stand by her for as long as you're able. And I will stand with you for as long as I'm able."

———

Two weeks after we closed the Auberge Rouge case, I found an apartment. The move in was simple. My three pairs of trousers and six shirts fit into a black trash bag along with the lone sweater, another pair of shoes, and Alba's turquoise belt. With my most recent paycheck, I bought a black wool overcoat. Brina gave me a blue wool scarf because she said it made my eyes shine.

The apartment was just six blocks from the Emerald Garden—far enough to give me a break when I needed one but near enough to not wear out my bum foot. Brina soon filled my new single-room apartment with jars of cuttings from the plants in her place. One night, at the end of a wrenching case, Brina arrived at my door with a sealed cardboard box. Inside was a tiny mewling ball of yellow fur. The kitten's eyes were a familiar gold, and its accusing stare was unmistakable.

"This is a housewarming gift from Mrs. Abernathy. She said her neighbor's cat had a litter two months ago, and they're pretty sure Peaches is the father."

I stuck a finger under the creature's chin for a closer study. "No doubt about it."

"Are you going to keep it?"

"I think so. I mean sure, why not?" I took the box from Brina and sat it on the floor and then tipped it over so the kitten could crawl out if it wanted.

"Got a name in mind?"

"I think I'll call him Herb." As if prompted by that decision, the kitten set one paw and then another out of the carton. He stared at me without a hint of fear in his yellow eyes.

"Any reason?"

"I don't know. Just sounds right to me." Explanations required a clarity I didn't possess, an optimism that still felt out of reach. I was steadier on my feet now than the morning I fled the Auberge Rouge fire. But the road ahead bent toward a horizon too hazy to describe with certainty. I wanted to say more, but Brina seemed satisfied with my sketchy response, and she let the kitten's antics turn our conversation in another direction.

Her early insight had proven true: Lots of people go missing in Harlem. The ones who want to be found get found. The rest, well, they stay lost.

I was one of the lost, but I'd been found by a cat, a job, a woman, and a neighborhood. As long as I was able, I would stand by all of them.

The End

Made in the USA
Coppell, TX
21 March 2020

17341367R00069